URIEL ...

A Whisper of Wings

Gilly Goodwin

CONTENTS

PRELUDE

*S*he's watching – keep digging! Hidden for a hundred years ... She said. You will be rewarded ... She said. *The grovelling wretch grunted and muttered his thoughts aloud as he dug around clumsily in the sand dunes, removing more and more sand from the hollow. He kept glancing around every few seconds, pushing his greasy hair back from his flat face, not wanting to take his eyes off the wisps of malevolent, inky smoke he'd seen spiralling from a nearby copse. *She's watching – keep digging. Deeper ... deeper, in an unfathomable pit ... it must stay hidden ... She said.*

Merrick was so preoccupied, he hadn't detected the piercing eyes studying his slow progress ... unblinking ... unwavering eyes. Nor did he notice a fair youth (concealed nearby), giving a secret hand signal.

Merrick sensed, rather than saw a hovering shape.

The gentle sound of brushing wings had always made him nervous, even waking him from nightmares in a cold sweat. He would lie shivering, glancing around from side to side, waiting ... waiting for an apparition ...

A heart-rending screech interrupted his black memories and a violent, frenzied beating of wings informed him that this was a new nightmare come to haunt him in real life. Sharp, needle-like talons skimmed past his head as a sea hawk, a large osprey, dived swiftly and with perfect aim for his right eye – guided like an arrow to its' target. It raked viciously with both claws and managed to slit the flesh open around the eye. Frantic waving and brandishing of the heavy spade managed to deflect the talons and so saved his sight.

There was a faint whistle and the osprey disappeared – job done. Uriel smiled faintly and carefully lowered himself back out of sight.

She's watching – keep digging.

Blood trickled down Merrick's right cheek and as he bent to dig, some of it dribbled into his other eye, rendering him almost blind. *This is deep enough. She won't notice. She daren't come this far into the sunlight. She's watching – keep digging.*

Merrick shivered, even in the warm sunlight. The black smoke was still swirling – a little closer now. He bent down, pretending the excavation was deeper than it was and grunting heavily, he managed to manoeuvre the heavy chest into the waiting trough. He left it interred, like an empty coffin in a sandy graveyard. He had done his best to bury it completely by replacing all the sand – but he knew ... it wasn't an unfathomable pit.

Did She know?

With a heavy heart, he shouldered his spade and limped awkwardly through the soft sand towards the menacing, shadowy smoke which was waiting impatiently; twisting and writhing with poison. He kept his eyes firmly on the ground, partly to check his faltering progress but also to conceal the guilt that he had not completely obeyed 'her' orders.

Buried ... deep ... deep? The words hissed and slipped into his thoughts almost as an order rather than a question.

She knows ... oh ... She knows! Merrick wiped the blood away once more and nodded his head slightly, not wanting to admit that he had disobeyed. He could just see the inky smoke, swirling in the extremities of his vision. *Don't look up, don't meet those eyes. She'll read your mind ... She will sense your guilt. Don't look up.*

He took a deep breath as the smoke drifted closer, swirling around his ankles and spiralling up and around his body. He shivered as it reached his chest and neck, almost covering him completely and blotting out the warmth of the sun.

Keep calm ... don't gag ... don't faint. She's hungry ... She's greedy. Stay strong. His senses started to fade as the smoke completely masked his face, and icy fingers slid into his mind, controlling his thoughts. Merrick was now completely swathed in a pillar of dark, rancid smoke, then – as though they had been sucked away in a whirlwind – Merrick and the phantom, disappeared.

CHAPTER ONE

The spaniel raced up and down the sand dunes, barking excitedly, her ears flapping like wings as she sprang from one hillock to another.

'Hey Bluebell ... ready-y-y ... fetch!'

The blue roan cocker spaniel froze in mid-pant. She watched carefully to see in which direction the damp piece of driftwood would be launched. Then, tongue lolling from side to side, she propelled herself after the missile.

Bud was top of the tallest dune – sending sticks into orbit for Bluebell, and gazing all around the almost deserted beach. Being so high up the dune, he smirked and glanced down with a feeling of maturity while watching his younger brother below. 'Hey c'mon what are you doing? ... Just how old are you, Blip?' he asked sarcastically.

His 12 year old brother Ricki, (known as Blip) was on the main part of the beach trying to walk backwards in the footprints he had made earlier. 'Hey! Bud – Batty – Watch me!' Blip tried to get their attention.

'Narrgh, you're just a blip on the horizon,' Bud teased him, but then looked down with far more concern at his sister. He called out gently, 'Hey – you ok?'

Batty (her nickname) was squinting closely at her phone, trying desperately to be able to see the screen in the bright sunlight. Her lips formed silent words as she finally managed to read her message and then threw her phone violently onto the sand and put her head in her hands. Her shoulders shook for a while until Bluebell dropped the stick at her feet and nudged at her with a wet, but very sandy, nose.

Bud clambered worriedly down from the highest sand dune and went to put his arm around her. 'Another one?' he asked, referring to the text message she had obviously just received.

Batty just nodded and Bud could see tears in the corners of her eyes. He sighed in exasperation knowing his little sister was having a few problems over friends at school – but knew he wouldn't be allowed to intervene as she wanted to *deal* with it herself. Batty was strong-willed, if slightly eccentric, and she didn't want to give in to the bullies making her life a misery at the moment. *No-one wants to be your friend ... just watch out...* Hmm.

She stroked Bluebell, whose nose was now pushed underneath her elbow in concern, and attempted to throw off the black mood which had overcome her usual high spirits. Batty stood up, took a good look around and suddenly yelled very loudly pointing towards the sea. 'Hey watch out! ... The tide's coming in!' She laughed in mock horror as her brothers both shaded their eyes from the sun and followed her line of pointing. 'Ha-ha, you two will believe anything!' The sea was in its usual place about three miles out.

Bud and Blip decided simultaneously to teach their younger sister a lesson.

'Get her,' yelled Blip.

'Cut her off!' ordered Bud as they both set off to catch her headlong flight over an uneven, undulating sand-dune. Bluebell thought it was a great game and ecstatically joined in. The brothers converged on their prey just as Batty disappeared behind a hillock. They all fell over the edge, got a mouthful of gritty sand and laughed uproariously while tickling Batty.

Suddenly Batty squealed in pain, a really high-pitched screech. Everything stopped. Even Bluebell's barking. Bud and Blip ceased tickling and moved away quickly; they were used to her short fiery temper. Bluebell whined in concern and nudged her arm, giving a small woof.

* * *

The Santorini family lived in South-Haven in Stanfordshire. That's a lot of S's ... but in the most significant parts of their lives, they found themselves gravitating towards other letters of the alphabet. Antonio and Antonia Santorini (second generation Italian immigrants, who ran a distinctive ice cream business) lived in a smart four-bedroom detached house in a typical Victorian seaside town which, in spite of having the name South-Haven, was in the north-west of the country.

Antonio and Antonia, known as "O" and "A" for obvious identification reasons, had decided there were too many names beginning with A in the family, and although they had chosen proper Italianate names for their off-spring – their eldest son, Nico, had very quickly been given the nickname of Bud as he had been a tiny premature baby and always fell asleep curled up, just like a bud! When he was old enough – and starting to unfurl (!) he had insisted that they should carry on calling him Bud instead of the more serious name of Nico ... even though he had grown into a lanky giant by the time he had reached his teens. The Santorini's had had two more children, Ricki and Gina, who very soon became widely known as Blip and Batty ... even beyond the family circle.

A few of the younger schoolteachers had started to use their family nicknames ... to the consternation of some rather naïve student teachers and the older more traditional staff.

'Why are you called Bud?' They would ask in a rather perplexed manner as their eyes were drawn upwards in curiosity at the tall youth.

'My name's Blip*aronio*,' exaggerated the cheeky, unkempt lad and he grinned at the rather urbane Head Teacher, 'but you can call me Blip for short.'

'Are you really called Batty?' Three young student teachers nervously watched the wide-eyed girl who was deliberately pulling a strange, anarchic smile, and asked in unison 'Why?'

So ... Bud had been a tiny baby, a little 'bud' cradled in his father's arms, with no promise of the long-limbed sapling to come.

Blip had been exactly that ... a blip on the horizon – an accident – a mistake. But Blip didn't care; he maintained that blips were important because they were always noticed.

Batty ... well, she was just that. Completely batty!

The three Santorini's had been taking advantage of a school inset day and were relaxing on the local beach, interspersed with frantic racing around the sand dunes, with their dog Bluebell barking excitedly ... until Batty had screamed. Bluebell's ears had immediately flopped and she whined pitifully, wondering if she had done something wrong.

'Ow! Help ... I'm bleeding ... I've cut my ankle on something.'

'Let's see!' Bud was a bit concerned as to what might be in the sand dunes on this part of the beach. It was a bit out of the way of regular beach-goers, but that meant that a few youths tended to congregate there at weekends.

'No, it hurts, it's bleeding a lot.' Batty was holding her ankle with both hands.

'Let me see,' insisted Bud. He managed to prise her hands away while she complained loudly.

'Oh Batty that's quite bad, it's bleeding quite a bit ... here have my hanky. Blip have you got yours?'

'I'm not using Blip's hanky,' stated Batty in horror. 'Have you seen it? I don't want to know where he uses it!'

Bud curled his lip in distaste, 'nor me!' Blip sighed and raised his eyes heavenward but for once didn't rise to the bait.

Batty used Bud's hanky to mop up the deep red blood trickling down her ankle. 'I wish it would stop bleeding,' she moaned, her voice breaking slightly.

'We'd better get you home. I wonder what you cut it on Batty. Let's have a look around in case it is dangerous.'

'Dangerous?' wailed Batty pushing her deep auburn hair out of her eyes.

She scrambled out of the way, ordering them to be careful and sat on a tuft of spiky marram grass. Bluebell joined her, trying to lick her ankle, while Bud and Blip gently trod around where Batty had fallen.

'It's somewhere around here, let's scoop some sand away but be careful of your hands, it might be sharp.' Bud instructed his eager brother.

'Of course it's sharp – you morons,' said Batty. 'It's made a deep cut, look I'm bleeding to death,' she stated melodramatically.

Blip stopped his excavating for a second. 'Can I have your goldfish if you die?'

'No you can't,' she said shortly. 'You should have looked after your own.' Then she added after a few seconds thought ... 'Goldfish don't like being taken to school for a day out ... particularly in leaky margarine containers!'

Bud snorted in amusement. 'We'd better get home before she bleeds all over the sand. Let's dig a bit deeper Blip, we need to be quick.'

'I wish it would stop,' repeated Batty mournfully.

They both resumed their cautious digging until Blip stopped and froze, 'Ha, what's this?'

'Let's see.' Bud moved closer and discovered a heavy piece of metal. He dug deeper and realised that the metal was attached to wood – a large piece of wood. Bud looked concernedly over his shoulder at Batty but Blip interrupted him just as he was about to speak.

'Let's keep going,' Blip said excitedly, 'we can be quick.'

'I wish it would stop bleeding!' repeated Batty a third time, starting to breathe more rapidly; feeling a little shocked. She winced as an abrupt flash, like an open window catching the bright sunlight, dazzled her for a second. Bud hesitated and was about to stop digging when he heard a startled sound behind him.

'It's stopped!'

'What?'

'It's stopped bleeding!'

'It can't have been that bad then can it? What a fuss.' Blip sounded exasperated.

'It was bad – you saw it – it was really deep.'

Bud went over to Batty and checked her ankle. 'It's not just stopped, the cut has almost disappeared,' he said peering closely at the wound. 'Odd.'

'But it was really deep,' insisted Batty.

'Well if you have finally stopped spurting blood everywhere,' announced Blip, 'it'll mean we've got time to dig this out. Let's keep going.' He was really keen to see what they had discovered. They all knelt down and tackled the problem with renewed vigour.

After a few minutes scraping and pushing the gritty sand out of the way, they paused and stared in awe at the uncovered object.

'Oh wow!'

'Oh cool!'

'Oh yes!'

'Woof!'

CHAPTER TWO

B atty breathed for them all. 'It is, isn't it? My God, it's an old treasure chest!'

'I wonder how long it's been buried.' Blip's eyes were as big as golf balls.

'I'm gonna open it,' Bud laughed at the glee and excitement written over their faces.

They all stared in awe at the old oak chest. It was a massive chest with a raised lid – bound together with thick iron bands. There were shiny brass rivets stamped in neat rows down each strip of iron.

They were so focused on the chest; they didn't see the ominous wisp of black smoke that slowly trickled over a nearby dune.

'It's a bit old – it looks as if it has been there for centuries,' breathed Blip, quivering with impatience.

'Let's just open it; it must have some kind of treasure inside.' Batty could visualise mounds of shiny gold coins.

The three of them, working together for a change, grunted and groaned as they put all their weight into trying to move the lid. It never budged. Not even with Bluebell's unwanted help.

Bud looked closely at the iron bands on the front. 'It must be locked ... look at that, it's an old keyhole.' They all stared with disappointment at the strangely shaped hole in the front.

'It looks like a diamond or maybe a kite shape,' Batty mused.

'Blip, go and fetch your old sledge so we can drag it back home. I don't want to leave it here now we've uncovered it and I certainly don't want the Wilton's to find it.' Bud pulled a face signifying his feelings about the so-called Wilton's.

Blip had disappeared before Bud had finished speaking. 'Yabba Dabba Dooooooooo!' came echoing back to them from the top of the dune.

'Bluebell – come here! Bluebell – come here!' Needless to say, Bluebell had decided to accompany Blip on his speedy journey.

While they waited, after fastening Bluebell to a large rock, Bud and Batty spent the time digging the rest of the chest out of the soft sand. When it was finally free, Bud walked all around it a few times inspecting each side. Batty sat down and rested her head on her fist, ruminating about what it contained.

By the time Blip reappeared, dragging his sledge and panting loudly, Batty had run through the whole gamut of what it might contain – including coins, some mouldy food, and then eventually, she decided it might contain ... er ... sand! Bud was trying to contain his temper and looked at Blip with relief.

'Thank God, come on, let's see if we can lift it – it's getting a bit dark now.'

It wasn't time to get dark, but a dank mist was rolling in off the sea and the light had taken on a sinister shade of grey. There was also a musty odour in the air around them.

'Time to go home folks,' Batty said simply as she noticed the approaching mist.

'Aargh! It's nearly teatime, come on quick!' Blip suddenly realised he was hungry.

They heaved and grunted and eventually slid the chest onto one side of the sturdy, plastic sledge, which immediately slid deeper into the soft sand. Bluebell climbed on top, barking encouragement – trying to help.

'Oh come on you stupid chest!' Bud panted with exertion. 'Blip, Batty, let's go and fetch some big flat pebbles.'

Bluebell also offered to collect some pebbles, getting completely in the way. Eventually after half an hour of trying, they managed to slip and slide the sledge off the dunes and towards the grass. They made more steady progress here as the ground was hard and the sledge managed to slide a little more easily.

As they left the beach, Batty heaved a sigh of relief and glanced over her shoulder at the advancing sea mist. Something didn't look right. It was too dark and shadowy and it moved strangely. Batty felt a shiver go down her back.

Just as they were very noisily trying to cross the only road that led to their house, disaster struck in the form of Mickey and Wayne – the two youths who had spent the past few years making the Santorini's lives a misery when they moved into the house opposite.

'It's the *Pantorini*'s! Listen to them!' Mickey laughed out loud, making fun of their surname.

'Hey it's that Scatty Batty!' Wayne pretended to fall over with uncontrolled hilarity.

'Oh look it's Bliparonio for ever on his ownio!' Mickey pulled Wayne up off the pavement and made rude gestures towards the three Santorini's.

Bud took a step forward with Bluebell growling at his side. 'And what are you going to call me?' He drew himself up to his full 14 year old height, which was actually the same height as a 17 year old being fed on plant fertiliser. Blip and Batty leant on the treasure chest and settled themselves down to watch any developments.

Wayne and Mickey ran around the side of their house. 'You're Bud the Dud!' came echoing back as Bluebell followed them barking madly. A large, sturdy wooden gate was slammed shut an inch away from Bluebell's nose. She gave a small indignant woof as if to make sure she had the last word.

Bud turned away with a rueful grin and walked back to the waiting pair, still lolling on the chest. 'Perhaps it's time to start using our proper names.' He put his head on one side ... looked quizzically at Blip and tentatively asked ... 'Blip*aronio*?'

Blip looked slightly embarrassed, gazed down at his feet and eventually described what he had said to the Headmaster – who refused to allow the use of nicknames. He explained that Mickey had been waiting in the Headmaster's office when Blip had cheekily announced his (mythical) extended name to Mr. Gamble. The door was open and Mickey had just been told that he was going to be kept down a year due to his lack of progress. He was now in the same year group as Blip, and making it very obvious he wasn't happy about it.

Blip sighed, 'I think I was the first person he saw after leaving the Head's office, and he decided to take it out on me ... ad infinitum! He keeps picking on me now.'

Bud asked again in total disbelief, 'Blip*aronio*? I bet Old Grumble enjoyed that one!' He gave the favourite school nickname of the irritable Head-teacher.

'Mickey just won't stop using the name.' Blip sighed, 'I wish they'd both go far away.'

Batty nodded her head in support. She was also fed up of 13 year old Mickey and his delinquent younger brother Wayne. Batty (who at ten years old, was about a year younger than Wayne) could usually stick up for herself, but recently, she had been feeling a little vulnerable and insecure. 'If only we could crush them in the bin lorry on Friday,' ... Batty thought out loud.

'Yay – squished Wiltons!' said Blip gleefully, making them sound like over-ripe fruit.

'Sounds a little violent,' remarked Bud.

'Oh Bud stop being a dud!' Blip ran around the other side of the huge chest in case Bud stretched out his extremely long arms and grabbed him by the ear. He was used to Bud's lengthy limbs and had often had his ear tweaked painfully.

'Hey, c'mon kids ... food!' Dad, otherwise known as Antonio, could be heard shouting from the back door. 'Where've you gone now?' he added in an exasperated voice.

'Coming Dad,' shouted Batty quickly.

'Come on! Let's get this chest inside without Dad seeing it.' Bud instructed the others and spurred them into action. They dragged the sledge around the opposite side of the house to where their Dad had been, but not realising just how much noise it had made.

'What on earth have you got there?' Antonio appeared around the back of the house, but Bluebell dived around him barking ecstatically and successfully distracted him. Luckily the chest was still out of sight around the corner of the house.

'We decided to try Blip's sledge on the dunes Dad ... to see if it was as good as in the snow.' Bud was a master at inventing on the spot. 'It wasn't!'

'Ok, get it put away quickly and into the house ... tea is ready and Mum is getting impatient.' Antonio added as an afterthought, 'Carbonara.'

'Yay, oh good, we'll be in now Dad.' Batty kept a look-out while the others grasped the sledge and dragged it to some open patio windows. These led into their play room known by all three B's as *the hive*. They struggled to place the heavy chest behind the interior door where it wouldn't be seen by adults, unless of course, they were particularly looking for it.

'We'll try to open it after tea,' Bud decided.

The three of them went to get cleaned up, all hopefully gazing backwards at the chest as they went through the door. Batty even patted it like a dog. Bluebell looked uncertainly at the chest, her tail quivering slightly and her ears drooping.

* * *

Tea was relaxed and enjoyable, once their Mum had had a few strong words about their time-keeping. 'Spaghetti doesn't like to be kept waiting,' she said sternly.

'Spaghetti doesn't know, Mum,' announced Batty rather sarcastically.

Antonia tried a different tack. 'And I want those goldfish cleaning out tonight ... straight after tea.'

'Oh Mum!' They all wailed in unison, their evening plans thwarted.

'Yes – tonight! Look they can hardly see through the tank because of all the algae. I have had to clear a little porthole for them to look out of,' she added wistfully.

'I don't have a goldfish now, so I don't need to clear out the tank do I Mum?' Blip reasoned.

'You can help.' Antonia was straight to the point.

Blip looked sadly at the two goldfish happily swimming around a large tank.

'I wish I'd got a goldfish.' he announced. 'It's not fair ... Batty has got Chrissy and Bud has got Clem,' he said referring to the unfortunately named Chrysanthemum and Clematis.

'Well that is because you didn't look after yours and tried taking it to school ... in a margarine container!' Antonia added – with a slight cough to disguise her amusement.

'You don't deserve one,' stated Bud.

'Well I still wish I had one.' Blip took another huge mouthful of Carbonara and was left with hot spaghetti tumbling all down his chin. 'Ouch!'

'Where are your table manners Ricki?' Antonio said sternly as Blip secreted a small piece of ham under the table to a patiently waiting Bluebell. Hot wet lips and a large red tongue practically sucked the ham and sauce off his fingers. There was a very small woof as a hint to the other children sitting round the table, but quietly enough to not annoy the adults.

When all had had their fill ... the Santorini version of Carbonara was cleared off the table, to be replaced with some ice-cream, fudge topping and a few strategically placed strawberries. The goldfish were forgotten, until the end of tea when Antonia reminded them of their task while she and her husband cleared the table.

'Come on,' said Bud 'it won't take us long if we all help.'

'Oh my God!' said Blip as Batty could be heard talking to her goldfish, Chrysanthemum.

'Hello Chrissy...' was all she managed to say before Bud and Blip interrupted her and explained there was no time to tell it a bedtime story. They quickly cleaned the tank, changed the water and scraped the glass panels. Blip was left gazing at Chrissy and Clem swimming around the newly cleaned rock formation and he sighed once again.

'I wish I had a goldfish,' he said wistfully.

'That is the third time you have said that now Blip, but you just can't be trusted,' announced Batty.

'Well I could be trusted to give it a better name than Clematis or Chrysanthemum.'

'But it would still have to follow the tradition ... begin with 'C' and be named after a plant,' stated Bud. 'What's wrong with calling it Cherryblossom again?'

Blip stuck his finger in his mouth and pretended to vomit. 'I'm not calling another goldfish of mine 'Cherryblossom' ... that was Mum's choice of name.' He paused. 'I could call mine Cactus,' then he added mischievously, 'I could shorten it to Ca...'

'Ricki!' a warning shot came from the kitchen.

Blip grinned at the use of his name and thought again. 'Ok ... how about Cowslip and I could call it 'Slip' for short?' Blip asked the question of the world in general but this time no answering shot came from the kitchen. 'Ok, Cowslip it is then!'

'But you haven't got one!' Batty was well known for stating the obvious.

They placed the hood back over the tank (ignoring the fluorescent bulb which had started to flash intermittently) and still arguing excitedly, they went to investigate their treasure chest. They carefully and quietly closed the door of the *hive* after them as they didn't want to be disturbed. A slight scratching at the door meant that Batty had to open the door again to let Bluebell satisfy her curiosity as to where they had all gone. They all sat around the chest and gazed at the keyhole. Bluebell sat down with them looking around expectantly.

'What can we do Bud? Where can we find a key that will fit?' Blip could hardly sit still he was so excited.

'I don't know,' said Bud. 'None of the house keys are old enough. It needs to be a really old-fashioned key, but it is also a really funny shape too. I've never seen a key that looked like that.'

Batty had her head on one side in puzzlement. 'What's that?' she asked.

'It's a keyhole Batty, something that needs a key to open it,' Blip was being sarcastic.

'No, not the keyhole ... that sound. What is it?'

They all went quiet, apart from Bluebell who decided to fill the void with some snuffles and whimpers as she investigated the strange smelly chest.

'Shush Bluebell,' they all said loudly.

'It sounds like something is slapping.' Batty leant towards the chest. 'It's coming from in there!' She looked a little wide-eyed with concern.

Bud and Blip moved closer to the chest and put their ears near the keyhole. Now they could all hear it clearly... a gentle, irregular slapping sound. Bud looked all around the playroom for some inspiration. 'What can we use to open it? There must be something inside.'

'I don't want to open it now,' Batty looked nervously at the others.

'Come on Bud, let's try brute force again,' suggested Blip flexing his puny muscles.

'Yeah ... Sparrows ankles!' laughed Bud using the family description of Blip's muscle growth.

'Knots in cotton,' Batty joined in, but with some trepidation. Her mind was on the chest.

Bud was doubtful it would work, but decided to show his strength off to the others. He went around the back of the chest and using his long arms to cover the top of the chest he grasped the lid.

'Wait for me Bud,' yelled Blip indignantly.

Too late! Bud had pulled with as much strength as he could muster. The lid flew open as easily as if it had been oiled, and crashed back against the wall of the playroom. Bud disappeared with a grunt behind the chest – banging his head hard against the chest lid and against the wall. 'For God's sake, it was locked before. I've really bashed my head now ... ow it hurts.' Bud wasn't happy, but his grumbling suddenly died away. 'What's the matter?' He peered over the lid and gazed upon his two siblings staring with wide-eyed astonishment at the inside of the chest. 'What's the matter?' he repeated.

'How... How ... How did that get there?' breathed Batty.

'It's mine. It's mine. It's mine – it must be!' Blip jumped up and down to punctuate each repetition.

Bluebell whimpered.

CHAPTER THREE

The inside of the chest looked huge – almost bigger on the inside than the outside. It looked completely empty and Bud wondered why on earth Blip was looking so excited. He pulled himself up onto his knees so he could see more clearly. It was an old, empty, dusty chest, but even as he looked – he could hear a small slapping sound and saw something moving out of the corner of his eye. He glanced upwards at Batty and Blip's faces gazing in awe at the bottom corner on the right. He struggled to stand up in order to see properly ... and ... slowly peeping over the lid, discovered ... a goldfish!

It was quite a big goldfish, but was very dusty and was getting more and more agitated as he gazed in astonishment. 'Quick! Blip! Get your hanky!' Bud shouted. 'Batty's still got mine!'

'Ugh!' stated Batty, referring to Blip's hanky.

'It's dirty Bud – it'll hurt it.' Blip was worried.

'The fish is already filthy dirty and covered with dust – your bathroom habits are not going to hurt it any more. It needs water and NOW!'

Blip squirmed, fumbled and furtled around for a bit and eventually extracted his dirty hanky from the depths of his pocket while Batty grimaced in distaste. 'Well where is your hanky?' he asked.

'In the wash,' she said piously.

Blip ignored her and scooped up the frightened goldfish. Bluebell suddenly became very interested and started barking loudly.

'Shush Bluebell – this is a secret,' Batty put her finger to her lips and Bluebell stopped barking and sat down immediately.

'Whoa! ... Have you trained her to do that?' asked Bud, surprised.

'I have lots of secrets,' hinted Batty by way of explanation.

Blip was creeping as carefully as he could towards the door. 'Someone open the door then!'

'Wait a minute Blip let me check the coast is clear.' Bud quietly opened the door and peered out. He waved to the others to follow him quietly and Batty signalled for Bluebell to keep it a secret once again.

As quickly and as silently as they could manage, they went to the lounge, happily finding it empty and opened the lid of the fish tank. There was a slight panic as Blip let the fish slip out of his hanky which landed with a resounding plop on the leather settee. Bluebell couldn't control herself and made a lunge with her wet jowls at the flapping, tasty morsel while all three of them leapt to the goldfish's defence. Blip managed to grasp it in his hot hands and drop it with a splash into the tank. They all fell about giggling and laughing with relief while Bluebell looked on in obvious consternation. She directed a little indignant woof at the tank.

After a short moment they started to control themselves and watched to see if the new addition to the tank was still alive. Clem and Chrissy were looking a bit surprised, but the newly named Cowslip was investigating the tank with interest. Their parents could be heard talking in the kitchen having finished the clearing up.

Blip, looking a bit dazed, asked ... 'Well how are we going to keep *that* a secret then?'

'It's Wednesday, they'll be visiting Nan soon and won't get back until later.' Bud tried to sound reassuring. 'Hopefully, they may not notice for a couple of days,' he added.

That night, before their parents returned home, they held a brief meeting in Batty's bedroom and were so full of questions they kept interrupting each other.

'Where did the fish ...?' 'How long had it been in the ...?' 'How could it still be alive?' 'Why was it in the chest?' 'Well ... how did the Chest know what Blip wanted?'

There was a sudden silence in the cosy bedroom.

'Well I made a wish for a goldfish, so perhaps it grants wishes,' laughed Blip, not really believing his own comment. 'Well how else did it get in there anyway?' he asked petulantly.

'Well if it grants wishes ... then I wish that your hanky was clean.' Batty giggled.

'Hey it's not a fairy story.' But Bud was really puzzled and feeling more than a little uneasy, so he decided to go to bed and sleep on it. 'Anyway g'night – need to get to bed. I've got a module and revision lessons tomorrow.'

Batty shut her door on her brothers and immediately her mood changed. She had tried to keep light-hearted in front of everyone, but her phone was burning a hole in her pocket and she wanted to read the texts which had kept vibrating every few minutes during tea. She sat on her bed and pulled the phone out. She scowled when she saw there were 5 texts waiting.

When she saw who had sent them, she knew what they would say, so she read them quickly, sighed deeply and turned the phone off.

She wished she didn't have to go to school the next day – but knew she had to face the problem and try to sort it out, rather than hide away. Batty climbed into bed, cuddled up in the duvet and wept a few anguished tears into her pillow. She thought how easy it would be if she could just *wish* the problems would go away.

✽ ✽ ✽

Thursday morning dawned warm and sunny, a beautiful, late spring day ... except that it was a school day. South-Haven School lay on a large site near the sand dunes, surrounded by green fields. On one side of the campus was the junior school with a small playground full of brightly coloured games painted onto the tarmac. The comprehensive school, for the senior students, was on the far side of the campus encircled by a grove of pine trees which helped to shelter it from the blustery coastal winds.

Two double-decker school buses carried some of the children to school; one from the local town area and the other collecting students from the outlying villages. Everyone else walked or cycled to school. The Santorini children didn't have far to travel and they could have walked, but the school bus conveniently stopped at the end of their street. The only downside to that was seeing Mickey and Wayne waiting at the same bus-stop.

This particular morning Mickey and Wayne had also arrived first, claiming the increasingly important status symbol – the wooden bench. Bud, Blip and Batty walked sullenly towards the bus stop. Their morning had not gone well. They had been questioned closely by an indignant and disbelieving Antonia. She was particularly disbelieving of Batty's attempt to tell her that Cowslip had been there for ages ... but that the tank had been so dirty she hadn't noticed it before! Then to top it all Blip discreetly tried to pull his hanky out to wipe up some egg yolk he had dripped onto a clean table cloth.

'Oh look Blip – it's *still* filthy!' wailed Batty, referring to the state of the grimy, dusty hanky without thinking. Antonia rounded on them all, berating them for spoiling her clean table cloth, for not putting their washing out – and for sneaking a new goldfish into the house without asking. They were sent out of the house with a flea in their ear and only a tiny wag from Bluebell whose ears were drooping even lower due to the raised voices.

They arrived at the bus stop to find Wayne and Mickey with their feet up on the wooden bench. Mickey smirked and Wayne pretended to wave while making yet another rude gesture with his hand. They whispered to each other and Blip was sure he caught the word *ownio!*

'I wish they would go away,' he whispered under his breath, but loudly enough for Batty to nod her head in agreement. His fist was clenched tightly around the dusty hanky hidden deep in his capacious pocket.

The double-decker bus roared up to the bus stop and the five children scrambled quickly on board. Mickey and Wayne were first, as tradition dictated that those who temporarily owned the wooden bench also got to the front of the queue. Bud climbed on with bowed head so he didn't brush it embarrassingly on the spittle decorated roof. He strode to the back of the bus as befitted his age and inside leg measurement, and sat in the centre seat so he could stretch his drain pipe legs half-way down the aisle.

Batty also climbed on with bowed head, a little subdued – but that was because she didn't want to meet the eyes of two of the other girls. She sat near the front and fastened her seat belt without a word. She tried to ignore the whispers that were just loud enough for her to hear. Spiteful whispers about her strange eccentric family; about her being over-confident; too clever for her own good; talking to herself because she didn't have friends. She took a deep breath and wished she was already at school where she had a number of general friends, but no ... not that one special friend, she thought ruefully.

Blip leapt on last, shoved Wayne out of the way, and impatiently followed Mickey upstairs to the front of the double decker. There he met his two partners in crime, Sandy and Stu... because in spite of Mickey's teasing ... Blip was rarely alone.

INTERLUDE

Clear grey eyes, stared through the dense, almost impenetrable bushes as Uriel lay hidden a few metres from the road.

His eyesight may have been clear – but Uriel shook his head gently as if to divert his mind from the confusion that still lingered. He was troubled by faint memories ... travelling through the forest ... answering a plea for help from Merrick and then sensing a faint, yet unpleasant aroma and struggling for breath. Uriel remembered seeing a faint curl of smoke twisting around the gnarled trunk of a tree and had soared into action to rescue the rather distasteful, grovelling youth. Then it had all gone black.

When he had eventually awoken from a deep trance, almost a state of hibernation – he'd felt dizzy and now recognised that he must have been benumbed by some kind of hypnotic vapour. He had felt empty and bewildered, his mind still cloaked and shrouded in mist ... except for the most disturbing dream ... *The secret chest had been stolen, and with it ... the most treasured and revered item hidden within.*

Uriel sighed in resignation as he recalled the day the chest had been interred in the dunes. The majestic sea hawk had been waiting – perched on a high branch, both vigilant and eager for Uriel's signal. Merrick had not fulfilled his task correctly and the osprey had been rewarded ... job done.

Uriel had been lying concealed in the dunes but once the unkempt servant had gone, he had uncurled his legs and stretched with relief. The early morning sun had been warming his back as it had climbed higher in the sky. After a few moments, he had wandered over to the dune and gazed down at the newly disturbed patch of sand. His mind had still been blurred and shrouded but he could just manage to sense the potential power radiating from the ground, reaching out to him ... yet still conveying an empty space.

He remembered peering around, contemplating the area. The sea had been a long way out, never approaching this section of the dunes. He had shaded his clear eyes from the glare of the sun and glancing in the opposite direction – he had seen nothing ominous there, just a few rooftops that signified the steady growth of a small seaside town.

He had been resigned to a lengthy wait and yet finally ... finally ... after restlessly pacing the isolated sand dunes for a number of years, he was now aware that *this* could be the advent of a new era. He watched carefully as the children approached the bus.

* * *

The three children were known to him. Protected ... safeguarded; yet he still had to wait for their decisions and the conclusions they reached concerning the chest. He had to trust their judgement.

They had revealed themselves to be a little eccentric and cheeky, yet for the most part ethically sound. They were concerned about their friends and family; they detested bullying yet weren't averse to having a bit of fun and didn't always follow the ground rules. They liked to stretch their boundaries ... in Blip's case ... almost to breaking point.

Today, Uriel observed them as they approached the school bus and he smiled wistfully at the interaction between their neighbours and themselves. Then as he watched, hidden from view, he noticed an ominous swirl of inky smoke seeping in through one of the open windows of the bus, before it pulled away.

Uriel shivered and frowned. This was the harbinger of evil ... a loathsome apparition meant to infiltrate the laughter of children and drain the soul of its generosity. It sought nourishment from exaggerated emotions which always threatened to overflow from youthful high spirits. It fed off life itself.

Uriel made his decision. He *had* to intervene when necessary ... even if it meant revealing himself in his true form.

CHAPTER FOUR

Mr. Gamble eyed the bus with misgiving. Hordes of loud, extravagant children streamed off the double-decker. They called out, teasing and insulting each other with their little foibles and eccentric mannerisms. He caught sight of a smallish, cheeky, red-haired lad following a tall, lanky beanpole who reached head and shoulders above the rest. Nico and Ricki Santorini ... otherwise known as Bud and Blip*aronio* he mused with a small, stressed chuckle. If he didn't laugh – he would cry!

At this point, he hadn't been introduced to Gina Santorini who still attended the junior part of the school. However, he had made a careful point of checking if the other two had any other siblings and was now in the process of deciding if his retirement should come before Gina reached the senior school on her next *rite of passage.* Mr. Gamble wasn't sure he had enough strength, particularly when he was informed her nickname was *Batty.* His forehead twitched at the thought and he walked slowly back into the school, his shoulders drooping.

Two hours later and Mr. Gamble was on the warpath, as gossip regarding Ricki Santorini had spread like wildfire. The rumours had already assumed gigantic proportions and the whole infamous episode was now known as *the great escape*.

* * *

After morning registration had been taken, Blip, Sandy and Stu had made their usual erratic journey down the corridors, pretending to trip each other up on the way. The three of them seemed to be incapable of walking normally. They soon came up behind Bud and his pals, who were ambling slowly as they discussed the latest sporting achievements by the local football team. Rushing to lessons was obviously beneath the Year 10 levels of maturity and it wasn't long before they had reduced the whole school to a tortoise pace as hundreds of impatient younger students bounced off the walls behind them in frustration.

'Year 10, keep moving – you are causing a traffic jam!' Mrs. Cresslyn's loud booming voice could be heard echoing down the corridor.

'Oh blast,' remarked Blip under his breath as he recognised his teacher's voice. He thrust his hands deep in his pockets and said mournfully ... 'Oh I wish I could go home.'

'What?' asked Stu.

'I wish I could go home,' he repeated.

'He doesn't mean it.' Sandy added ... 'do you Blip?'

'I wish I could go home, or get sent home anyway ... and then I wouldn't have to face Miss!' He looked a little frustrated. 'Oh no, think ... quick!' he announced to no-one in particular.

Sandy and Stu assumed he was referring to himself as neither acolyte practised thinking too deeply anyway. The strip lights in the corridor suddenly flickered a few times. Blip froze like an ice-sculpture and came to a dramatic, sudden halt in the crowded corridor. He dug his elbows into other students trying to push past him and then suddenly smiled in glee. 'Hey boys, watch the master at work!'

In an instant, Blip changed from a cheeky, grinning red-headed squirt of a boy to a doleful, solemn and tearful wretch. Blip vigorously rubbed his eyes. Tears began seeping from beneath his reddened eyelids and his lower lip trembled with distress. Sandy and Stu looked quickly at him, intrigued by the sudden change – but then noticed a slight lowering of one eyelid in a wink.

Mrs. Cresslyn, preparing for a fraught Year 8 English lesson on Romeo and Juliet was abruptly brought back to the present day as an unusually quiet Blip, edged in slowly through the open doorway.

'Blip – er Ricki, whatever is the matter?' she asked resignedly.

Blip's bottom lip quivered and he looked ready to burst into tears. He began to stutter 'Miss... um... er... Miss, *you* wouldn't blame me for something I hadn't done,' his tearful voice broke, 'would you Miss?' Blip took a deep breath and gulped 'I know I'm naughty sometimes Miss, but if I really hadn't done it – YOU wouldn't blame me would you Miss?' Blip pleaded with the harassed English teacher.

Mrs. Cresslyn eyed him with horror as he tugged his grimy handkerchief from an intimately placed pocket and started to vigorously wipe his eyes. A cloud of fine, white dust wafted from the hanky and landed on the side of her desk. She distractedly wiped it off with her hand. 'Can you really promise me that you haven't done anything?' Mrs. Cresslyn asked tentatively.

'I promise Miss!' Blip nodded emphatically. 'I haven't done it!'

'Well then you will need to explain to the person who is accusing you just why you feel you haven't done it – but I can personally assure you that I won't blame you or accuse you Blip – er Ricki.' Mrs. Cresslyn finally felt in control.

Blip grinned suddenly and made sure he had a full audience ... 'Ok Miss,' he paused dramatically ... '*I haven't done my homework!*'

The class erupted into uncontrollable laughter. Sandy fell off his chair and landed on the floor clutching his stomach in agony. 'Oh stop it. Please stop it – my sides hurt!'

Stu joined him sprawling on the floor, a little melodramatically, Mrs. Cresslyn thought.

She turned away, partly because she was ostensibly counting up to twenty in order to calm her simulated anger, but also because she was also grinning from ear to ear. The cheeky brat! She faced the unruly class – who were still applauding and cheering Blip's virtuoso performance. Mrs. Cresslyn took a deep breath and made sure she projected her voice over the continuing hilarity.

'Right year 8's ... Act 3 ... Ricki you can take the part of Tybalt ... he gets *murdered* in this act,' she announced threateningly.

'Yes Miss, Ok ... I get the message Miss.' Homework wasn't mentioned again.

An hour or so later, Blip was fidgeting outside the Science lab while his class were still inside, continuing with their lesson. Blip thought it was really unfair this time as he had only been using his initiative. He had pulled off a small piece of rubber and bunged it up the spout of a dripping tap. It wasn't his fault that Professor Cresslyn (Mrs. Cresslyn's grumpy husband) had just instructed Stu to fill a glass beaker with cold water from the same tap. Stuart had enthusiastically turned the tap on full, which had violently spurted water out horizontally and drenched all the nearby students. A loud stentorian voice could be heard cutting through the girlie screams and various shouts of ...

'Oh Blip!'

'Why did you do that?'

'Stop it Blip!'

'Turn it off Stu!'

'Mop it up with something!'

'Put your hanky away Blip – it's filthy!'

'YOU... BOY! You ... What's your name? ... Ricki! Go and wait outside!'

The room fell silent while Blip slid off his lab stool and ambled slowly to the door. Stu and Sandy were trying to explain to Prof. Cresslyn that it wasn't Blip's fault and that he had only tried to stop the dripping tap. The excuses fell on deaf ears, but it meant that the class (and professor) were distracted for a few moments as Blip, grabbing his bag from the bench near the door, suddenly realised the strap had dislodged one of the sand pots from the base of the nearby locust cage. He took a quick, surreptitious look around, but the class was too engrossed in Stu and Sandy's explanation as to why Blip shouldn't be punished. He began to retreat ... sand pot grasped in his hand, while glancing with fascination at the apocalyptic insects jumping closer and closer to their escape hatch. He discreetly made his escape, threw the sand pot in a nearby bin and stood outside the door holding his breath.

He chuckled to himself as the rather well-built Science Technician with the celebrated nick-name of *Matilda the builder,* entered the lab with a tray full of washed beakers and test-tubes. (The rather infamous name had originated from a story, that one of the prefects was reported to have seen her carrying a stack of six wooden lab stools on one shoulder).

It was later quoted on various messaging sites that... some of the escaping locusts had jumped on Matilda's hair... her screams had been as loud as the fire alarm... and that they had even reached the correct decibel to have shattered two glass beakers on the tray. A few killjoys had argued this wasn't possible, but their comments had been quickly drowned out by the countless rumours; and presumably by Matilda's hysterical screams.

Blip had feigned complete innocence when he had immediately been hauled up in front of Mr. Gamble. 'Me sir - No sir!' he had announced in answer to a few pertinent questions. 'I wouldn't do that sir!' he denied the possibility completely, while crossing his fingers behind his back.

'Then would you like to explain how the CCTV cameras (Mr. Gamble indicated the screen on his computer) have filmed you coming out of the Science lab with what looks suspiciously like a locust's sand pot in your hand?' he asked pointedly.

Blip looked accusingly at the screen. 'When did you get those installed sir?'

'Stop changing the subject. The sand-pot was found in the bin... and we both know who put it there – *don't we?*' asked the headmaster impatiently.

'Er... yes sir' Blip stared at his shoes pretending to be shame-faced – but in fact he still thought it had been worth it just to hear *Matilda the builder's* screams.

Blip concluded that the impromptu escapade had really paid off for him when he was excluded for the rest of the day and sent home ... that is ... until his Dad had picked him up following an angry phone call from the head teacher. Their conversation on the way home could hardly be described as amicable and Blip found himself grounded for the next week.

The rest of the school day passed without any other startling interruptions, but the journey home on the school bus seemed to be overflowing with amused and boisterous students discussing the day's events with excited voices. The rumour mill was now starting to work full tilt. Certain key words and comments could be heard at various points of the journey.

'Blip?'

'He did *what?*'

'No ... really ... *Locusts?*'

'Matilda the builder did *what?*'

'How? ... Where?'

'Wicked!'

Bud no longer sat with his legs stretched out in front of him like two immature saplings. They were almost folded up, whilst he sat uncomfortably on the edge of his seat in an earnest conversation with his friends. Late that morning, they had all been engrossed in a poetry set-text lesson with Mrs. Cresslyn, when a reading of Wilfred Owen's *Strange Meeting* had been rudely interrupted by vibrant, piercing screams and a rush of feet in the corridors.

'What the hell was going on? How did it happen?' Pete giggled, shook his head in disbelief then added, 'You were closest to the door Levi – did you see any more than we did?'

'I couldn't believe my eyes!' Levi tried to explain while trying hard not to laugh. 'Three locusts jumped down the corridor chased by Prof. Cresslyn.'

'All I saw was Mrs. Cresslyn raising her eyes heavenward and muttering under her breath,' remarked Michaela with a huge grin. 'I think she was saying something like, 'Oh no not *again!*''

'Was she referring to her husband ... or the escaped locusts?' Bud asked with some sarcasm.

Meanwhile, Batty was keeping her head turned away, yet listening carefully to the whispers from other junior students across the aisle.

'Did you hear what happened in the senior school?' Raine's cruel mouth pouted and then smirked back into its usual position. 'Her brother got excluded,' she laughed spitefully.

'I heard he let all the locusts escape!' Francine (known as Frankie) giggled relentlessly.

Raine glanced sideways across the aisle and said in a stage whisper, 'It's a shame that Batty doesn't get herself excluded, and then it would be quieter around here. She's always talking ... to herself!' she laughed spitefully.

'She's got no-one else to talk to,' smirked Frankie. 'So she has to talk to herself!'

Batty turned and looked out of the nearby window, trying to pretend she hadn't heard any of the spiteful comments. She blinked her eyes a few times as a lonely tear seeped from one lower eyelid. The ache in her heart was unbearable at times.

Up on the top deck, Sandy and Stu eyed each other with concern. 'Well he said he wanted to go home ... but I thought he was joking,' said Stu.

'Blip's i-in trouble – Blip's i-in trouble,' sang the entire top deck.

'It wasn't Blip's fault,' Sandy shouted back.

The journey continued, still causing various types of discomfort for the two remaining Santorini's, until the bus approached their stop. Batty pretended to skip off the bus, but her expression was more downcast than usual. Bud loped off and gave a friendly wave to his pals still sitting on the back seat. He was followed by a jeering Mickey and Wayne, but he wasn't in the mood to retaliate.

Bluebell, who had spent a large part of the afternoon looking puzzled and rather bereft at the bottom of the stairs, cheered up when the other two arrived home, but those big brown eyes still looked rather wistfully at Batty who patted her reassuringly and stroked her soft muzzle. She just couldn't understand why Blip had come home early and then had spent the entire afternoon in his room. Bud and Batty quickly changed out of their uniforms and into more comfortable jeans and went back down the stairs. Their parents were talking in the lounge but they went quiet when the two of them entered the room and Antonio asked them to call Blip down for tea.

The atmosphere at tea was a little uncomfortable. Blip was sulky, their parents were obviously disappointed and although they had expected Antonia to launch into one of her incessant sermons – she had refrained from commenting about school and had channelled the conversation with her husband towards work matters. Obviously everything else had been said earlier in the day and Bud and Batty glanced occasionally at Blip who, for the most part, remained mute.

The "B" meeting in the hive was full of questions and a few quiet giggles. They all sat around the chest using it as a focal point in the cluttered room. Bluebell lay with her head resting on Batty's knee. Bud's knee was too bony and Blip was too fidgety.

'C'mon tell all ... what happened, Blip?' Bud set the ball rolling.

'Nothing... Nothing... Honestly!' Blip shook his head, but couldn't meet their eyes at all.

'Come on Blip! We've all heard the rumours and that it was you who got sent out of the room as a punishment ... again!' Batty added with feeling and stared at Blip who was fidgeting in discomfort. 'But to get yourself excluded ....'

'Well I didn't do it on purpose. It wasn't my fault that I got sent out and the sand pot had just come loose ... so I just helped it along a bit ... and out through the door!' He added with a grin. 'I know I wished to go home earlier in the day, but how was I to know that Old Grumble was spying on me?'

Bud did his best not to grin at Blip. 'The locusts reached the English corridor,' he said holding his breath with difficulty. '... The screams reached the moon!' he added.

Blip snorted and Bud's resolve to be serious gave way to mirth and they both rolled around the floor to Bluebell's excitement.

Batty stretched out and gently touched the chest in front of her. Her thoughts were wandering. She had been watching Blip carefully and suddenly asked 'You actually made a wish to go home?'

Blip eventually swallowed, breathed deeply and stuttered, 'Y–Yes, I did, but only because I hadn't done my homework for Mrs. Cresslyn. I like Mrs. Cresslyn ... she's cool!' Blip thought for a moment, 'but what has that got to do with anything? We've all had fun making pretend wishes and the others weren't granted'... Blip paused ... 'except for the goldfish,' he added in a puzzled tone.

Bud laughed. 'So why was this one granted – if you actually did make a wish Blip?'

Batty quietly asked an extra question. 'How many times did you say it Blip?' But the question was lost in the sudden excitement as, simultaneously, Bud and Blip came to an inevitable conclusion.

'It must be the chest – it must be, Bud! It *does* grant wishes!' Blip's eyes shone.

Bud frowned as he looked at the chest. 'Well I'm not entirely convinced, but if so, why does it grant some wishes and not others?' Bud paused in thought for a while and then tried to answer his own question. 'Perhaps it only grants wishes if you really mean them, and that's why it didn't grant Batty's wish about your hanky, Blip...'

'But I *really* meant the wish about Blip's hanky,' interjected Batty.

'...but then it punishes you if you don't ask for a 'good' wish.' Bud ignored Batty and finished his sentence.

'How has it punished me?' Blip almost laughed again.

'Haven't you been grounded Blip?' Batty asked pointedly.

Blip looked a little stricken. 'Oh ... I never wanted to upset them. I just fancied a day off without getting told off about my homework.' He thought for a few seconds...'I know, I'll make another wish and put it right.'

'No you won't!' Bud and Batty said in unison.

'You would make it even worse.' Bud slapped the top of the chest making Bluebell jump. She barked loudly, but Bud ignored her as he came to a more sensible decision. 'We need to work out what is really happening first, *before* we make any more wishes.'

'Ok Bud.' Blip sighed, but eventually agreed. He reached out a hand and touched the chest longingly. Batty stayed silent for once but the others didn't notice.

Later that night, Blip thought he heard a door open surreptitiously, but presumed it was someone going to the bathroom so he just turned over to face the wall, going back over the day's events in his mind.

* * *

Friday morning and Batty, unusually, was up bright and early and was actually going out through the door as Bud and Blip hurriedly arrived for their breakfast, still trying to fasten their ties – an almost impossible task to complete when eyes are still half-closed.

'I'll get to the bench first today. Hurry up and eat your toast you two, I don't want to be on my own with Mickey and Wayne.' Batty seemed quite excited as she slammed the door after her.

'What's the matter with her?' Blip was sounding a bit moody even though it was a Friday morning. He was a little worried as to what would actually happen at school. 'She's not even dressed properly,' remarked Blip, 'and she has her ponytail tucked down inside her coat. She hasn't even done her hair properly.'

'Well you can talk, Blip,' Bud eyed his younger brother, 'your tie is outside your collar and your *strawberry blond hair*,' he said pointedly, 'is sticking up like an embarrassed hedgehog!'

'Ha yes, very funny,' Blip tried to make his voice as scathing as possible. They swiftly left the house followed by remonstrations from Antonia who had just seen the state of the breakfast table. Once safely in the street Blip dragged his feet all the way to the bus stop.

'Hey it's *slippy* Blippy,' the dreaded voice of Wayne penetrated the black fog that had engulfed Blip's usual good nature.

'Oh shut up!'

The perpetual daily bus arrived and Bud found himself following Batty up the steps, curiously noting that she still had her long ponytail tucked inside her coat – when she came to a sudden halt, grunting loudly as Bud pole-axed her, almost causing a whiplash injury. He expected a mouthful of sisterly abuse but she just stood still in the middle of the aisle, frozen into immobility. Blip lost patience, pushed Bud's arm out of the way and elbowed Batty in the ribs.

She still didn't move... someone was sitting in her usual seat.

CHAPTER FIVE

A petite, fair-haired girl smiled shyly at Batty. 'I'm sorry, have I taken your seat? I didn't know and no-one answered me when I asked.' She spoke quietly with a clipped accent that Batty couldn't place.

'That's all right,' said Batty. 'Can I sit here too? Are you starting today?'

'Yes to both,' she said quietly. 'I don't know anyone and Táta just put me on the bus in town. I'm feeling a bit lost,' her voice broke slightly.

'Táta?' Batty asked gently. 'I'm Gina by the way – otherwise known as Batty.'

'Táta is my father,' said the girl in answer, although she was rather puzzled by Batty's name. 'Batty?' she asked shyly.

'Don't ask! What's your name?'

'Lenka,' she added by way of explanation... 'It means 'light.' I am from Prague.'

At that moment the sun burst through the clouds and shone through the bus window onto the two girls.

For Batty and for Lenka, the day just got better. By lunchtime, they were firm friends, in spite of the sarcastic comments and smirks from Raine and Frankie and a few other girls in their class. Batty had found a friend and she was always going to be loyal. She even trusted her new friend enough to confide in her and they could be seen huddled on a bench while Batty slipped her coat down over her shoulders. Lenka was seen to smile broadly and stroke the ends of Batty's long wavy ponytail. She also showed Lenka the treasured item in her skirt pocket and her new friend was satisfyingly impressed.

For Blip, the day got worse. He spent the entire morning wondering when the summons would come from Mr Gamble. He couldn't believe he had only been excluded for part of one day and wondered what other punishment would be forthcoming. He soon found out after lunch ... when he had his next Science lesson with Prof. Cresslyn.

'Ah ... Ricki Santorini...' announced the professor with what seemed unnecessary and inappropriate glee.

'Yes sir,' Blip answered rather tentatively.

'Well, you s-seem to be my lab helper for the foreseeable future, Ricki.' Prof. Cresslyn snarled with almost cat-like fervour. 'Mr. Gamble's instructions ... You can start by feeding all the locusts ... then the gerbils ... then the African toads.' Professor Cresslyn glared at Blip. 'Then you can help the technicians prepare *all* the equipment for next week. Make sure you close ALL the cages, securely,' he warned, a little belatedly.

Blip was kept busy, including missing the last lesson of the day – his favourite gym lesson.

* * *

Friday afternoon was usually a time to meet in town after school, so Bud continued on the bus with his pals, intending to eat tea at a local burger bar. Blip, Sandy and Stu all got off the bus at Blip's usual stop and went to spend some time on the beach, ignoring Mickey and Wayne's comments following them down the road. Batty went a few streets further than usual in order to call at the local shop, where she needed to buy something important ... she said.

Batty waved to Lenka who still had to travel into town and tried to ignore her elder brother Bud, who had suddenly decided to remind her to make sure she got home in time for tea. He was yelling through a high open window as Batty shook her head at him and turned to go towards the shop. As she did so, her ponytail flipped out of her coat and Bud was left speechless as he noticed all the tips of her hair were... green!

'Wow,' said Michaela. 'When did she get that done?'

'She didn't. It was dark auburn yesterday... *I think*,' added Bud, perplexed.

Levi laughed. 'Do you think I could get away with green streaks of hair under my yarmulke?'

'You only wear it at the synagogue, don't you?' asked Michaela. 'What would old Grumble say if you turned up to school with green hair streaks?'

'Well what are "A" and "O" going to say about *green hair?*' Bud asked the world in general.

'I never did understand why you call your Mum and Dad, "A" and "O".' Pete shook his head in wonder.

'Everyone calls them "A" and "O" so they don't get confused with their proper names.' Bud defended his eccentric family.

Michaela laughed, 'Hey if they had another child, what "B" nickname would they use then?'

The bus pulled away and continued its journey into town while almost everyone on the bus (Bud thought) had to give their own ideas of "B" nicknames.

'Bagel,' came from Levi.

'Baked Bean,' was gleefully suggested by Michaela.

'Butthead!' ... that was Pete.

Other names included Banana, Blob, Bamboo, Beetroot and Buttercup – but by this time Bud had put his headphones back in his ears and was ignoring all comments.

* * *

Batty walked down the road to the shop and asked for a voucher to put some credit on her new, secret, 'state-of-the-art' phone. She knew she had saved up enough money for a decent amount of air time. She then spent the next ten minutes walking slowly along the pavement, holding her phone in front of her, getting more and more frustrated as she tried in vain, to make it work.

She gradually became aware of a small figure in front of her, almost bent double and groaning loudly. 'Mrs. Smythe!' she called as she recognised the old lady in difficulties. 'Are you ok? Can I help you?' Batty knew Mrs. Smythe as a kind hearted but timid old lady who sometimes slipped her a bar of chocolate or a small amount of pocket money if she ran any errands for her in the holidays. Mrs. Smythe gasped with relief as she saw Gina who lived two doors away from her.

'C-can you help me home dear? I'm not feeling too well.'

'Yes of course,' Batty abandoned her efforts with her phone and quickly took Mrs. Smythe's arm.

'Oh gently dear ... go slowly please.' She gasped in pain and Batty began to look more and more troubled as she helped the lady towards her home. Batty was only a year 6 student and in spite of her usual maturity, she was really feeling out of her depth in this situation. Mrs. Smythe's face was as white as a sheet, apart from a blue tinge around her mouth and Batty started to get really worried. She knew the lady lived alone and there was no-one else to look after her.

'Mrs. Smythe can I get a doctor to you – or an ambulance?' she added.

At that point Mrs. Smythe's rather bloodshot eyes drifted up in her head and she collapsed. Batty really panicked and tried to break her fall, but she just wasn't strong enough and Mrs. Smythe landed on the pavement with a bump.

'Mrs. Smythe! Mrs. Smythe!' called Batty, but there was no response. Batty remembered that even though she had not managed to put any money on her phone, it should still make emergency calls. But she had never made one and was rather nervous of doing so. She looked all around for help, but in spite of it being a Friday afternoon, she was in a fairly secluded area and was completely alone with the rather huddled, shapeless figure on the pavement.

She took out her phone and tried to turn it on. No signal. She ran up a small grassy bank and tried again. Signal, thank goodness! The phone charged up and she pressed the emergency button – nothing. There was just no response. Her new, treasured phone was not working. In fact, it hadn't worked since she had it – and she was quick-witted enough to realise in dismay just why it was *never* going to work. She threw it on the pavement in frustration.

Batty hardly noticed a distant rumble of thunder a few miles away, but she felt a sudden change in the atmosphere and looked warily around. She had heard a strange rustle in the bushes nearby. Was someone hiding? Could she hear a faint sound of breathing? What was it? Batty realised she didn't want to turn her back to the bushes. She looked intently through the leafy branches ... could she see a pair of eyes ... piercing, unblinking eyes?

Mrs. Smythe was still lying huddled on the ground and Batty started yelling and shouting in panic; not wanting to leave her – but desperate to summon help. After a few minutes, her voice getting husky, a small figure and a dog appeared at the top of the road. Thank goodness ... it was Blip, home early from the beach, taking Bluebell for her teatime walk.

'Blip ... Blip ... BLIP!' She shouted as loudly as she could and Blip realising something was wrong, eventually came running, with Bluebell barking excitedly alongside.

'What's the matter? What's wrong ... who's this?' Blip looked in alarm at Batty and then at the forlorn figure on the pavement.

'It's Mrs. Smythe, she's collapsed. You need to use your phone and get help.'

'OK,' he said, quickly pulling his phone out. Then Blip paused, 'Why haven't you used your own phone?'

Batty indicated her phone on the ground and said, 'It's not working.'

Blip phoned for the emergency services and looked down at Batty's phone while he was waiting for the call to go through. 'That's not your phone... that's one of the new models... you can't have one of those... "O" will never pay for that.' His stuttering phrases were interrupted by the call centre and he had to concentrate in order to give them the correct details. Meanwhile, Batty picked up the errant phone and surreptitiously put it back in her pocket.

Luckily, a locally-based paramedic arrived in a few minutes, followed shortly by the ambulance. Mrs. Smythe was taken safely off to hospital after the paramedics had asked a few questions and made a few checks. Blip and Batty both heaved a sigh of relief and started to walk a confused, yet excited dog, back up the slight incline. Batty kept swivelling her head around nervously, in order to stare at the bushes and Blip, now walking behind her after pausing to pick up the inevitable *gift* from Bluebell, suddenly noticed her hair.

'What in God's name is that?'

Batty was lost in her thoughts and her mind was elsewhere. 'What is what? ... Oh that! I just dyed the tips of my hair.' She hoped her matter of fact response would stop the comments, but then Bud leapt off a bus at that precise moment and very quickly started to join in with Blip's astonished and rather searching questions.

She tried to change the subject. 'Why are you back for tea Bud – I thought you were having tea in town?'

'The weather is changing haven't you noticed? I shouldn't be surprised if we're going to get a thunderstorm soon, so I decided to come home before I got drenched.'

Batty started to walk ahead as quickly as she could; hoping that any further questions and comments would stop, as she was feeling really uncomfortable and confused about the whole problem. She wanted somewhere quiet so that she could think things through.

Mickey and Wayne suddenly appeared at the corner of the road, which interrupted the flow of comments and questions from Bud and Blip. Batty stopped, waiting for the others to catch up.

'Hey, look who's here!' Wayne and Mickey crossed the road to greet them in their own sneering way and Mickey directed a gob of spit towards Blip's feet.

'Oh no ... not again,' said Blip under his breath and then mumbled a few extra uncouth comments.

Bluebell barked angrily and Wayne swiftly decided to cross back over the road.

Mickey stood his ground. 'Is that green snot on your hair, Batty? Been picking your nose? Why don't you go ginger like Blip? Hey Bud ...what's the weather like up there? Going to be a storm soon, watch out for the lightning!' Mickey then swaggered back over the road towards Wayne, who had been listening and chortling with total respect at his elder brother's comments, while still keeping a wary eye on Bluebell. The spaniels' nose had started to wrinkle in warning and she was snarling in Wayne's direction, showing him an alarming set of teeth.

'Oh I really do wish they'd go far ... *far* away.' Blip tried to control his temper by ramming his fists in his pockets and then dragging a growling and bristling Bluebell back home.

Bud was about to take a step towards Mickey and Wayne when a dazzling flash of lightning, followed swiftly by a huge clap of thunder, made him turn on his heels and lope quickly in the direction of home. The others had already vanished into the house.

CHAPTER SIX

After a fraught teatime, Bud and Blip decamped to the *hive* quite a bit earlier than Batty. Firstly she had had to endure an extremely long and incessant telling off from "O" and "A".

'It was worse than a sermon,' she remarked tearfully as she later recalled all the ethical arguments that had been used in response to her "inconsiderate selfish actions." She was then dragged off after tea, to have her hair washed and when that didn't remove the green "snot" (as it was now referred to by Blip) she had also had to endure having her hair trimmed so that it left only slight traces of green.

When she finally arrived for the "B" meeting hoping for some support from the others, she was looking troubled and was unusually quiet. Bluebell snuggled up to her as she sat down, a little further from the chest than usual. She stroked the dog's head gently and Bluebell licked her hand reassuringly, sensing she was upset. The room was quiet for a time, apart from some ominous growls of thunder which were then echoed by Bluebell.

Eventually Bud sighed and said, 'We need to talk.'

'It wasn't me today,' insisted Blip, raising his hands in innocence. But Bud wasn't accepting any excuses.

'We need to talk about *all* of it – tonight. We need to work out what is happening before someone really gets hurt.'

It all went really quiet. There was a distant flash, but no thunder.

Batty realised she had to get the ball rolling and she took a deep breath. 'It ... it d-does grant wishes,' she stammered, referring to the chest. Her voice broke into a sob ... 'but you have to ask for it at least 3 times. To make sure you really mean it, I suppose.'

'Blip tried to pull his hanky out, 'well look, it didn't clean my hanky,' he said proudly, as a cloud of dust flew off the filthy piece of cloth that finally emerged from his pocket.

Bluebell's nose quivered as she first sniffed the proffered hanky, then the dust and then snorted uncontrollably.

'We didn't ask for that three times,' said Batty quietly. There was silence again while Blip and Bud assimilated what she had just said.

'How do you know this Batty? I hadn't worked that out.' Bud was doubtful.

Batty stretched her leg out and pushed her sock down to reveal her ankle. 'I guessed it was something to do with the number of times we made a wish, after my ankle healed and the goldfish appeared from nowhere. I couldn't believe it.' she added.

'Neither could I.' Bud shook his head in disbelief, referring to the amazing entrance of *cowslip*.

Batty continued... 'So I decided to try it out and I came downstairs last night to wish for some things I really wanted.' She paused. 'My hair, a new phone and...' She hesitated and then with her voice trembling a little, she quietly said, '... and a friend ... it worked,' she said baldly, a few seconds later.

Bud touched her knee gently. 'I knew you were having some problems ... but I didn't realise how much,' he said referring to the friend issue. 'I'm sorry I didn't try to help, you usually seem so strong.'

Blip had been thinking carefully. 'I *think* I wished to get sent home *three* times ... but I wasn't anywhere near the chest when I made the wish, I was still at school.'

Bud looked down at the fine light dust from Blip's hanky that was still scattered on the carpet near the chest. 'Well I might have the answer to that... look at the dust! Blip your hanky is so dirty it still has some dust on it from when you rescued the goldfish out of the chest. The dust must belong to the chest, so ... when you made your wishes you were still *close* to the chest, or perhaps that even counts as ... *touching* the chest.'

'I think it might have been teaching you a lesson too,' Batty sighed.

'As I said before, maybe it punishes us if we don't ask for sensible or *good* wishes,' said Bud.

'But *your* wishes worked well, didn't they?' Blip asked Batty curiously.

'The tips of my hair turned green, yes. But look at it now it has been cut. So that didn't work out well for me, did it?' Batty said somewhat bitterly. 'I am grounded for weeks now.'

'Me too,' sighed Blip. 'What about the smartphone?' Blip was jealous as he knew he would never be allowed that particular model.

'It wouldn't work at all. It wouldn't take my voucher. It wouldn't even register an emergency call.' Batty looked up at Bud with tears in her eyes. 'It meant I put Mrs. Smythe's life in danger. My old phone would have worked, but I was just showing off and wanted a new phone.' She stopped and thought. 'So, perhaps you were correct when you said the chest punished us if we didn't ask for "good" wishes.'

'Well it seems to have accepted your ankle...' he said, counting on his fingers ... 'the goldfish, unless Cowslip suddenly decides to eat Chrissy and Clem, and... your new friend?' Bud glanced at Batty for corroboration and she smiled wistfully in agreement. He then continued... 'And it seems to have *punished* us for ... *the great escape*,' he glanced at Blip and tried not to grin ... 'and your hair and your phone, Batty.'

Blip wriggled in discomfort. 'The real question is not that we've been punished, if that is the case ... but *how* can we put some things right?' he said, thinking of his exclusion and the problems Batty had when her phone didn't work in an emergency situation.

A huge drumroll of thunder rolled around at precisely the same moment as a double flash of lightning. The storm was now right overhead. In the silence that followed, a loud forceful knock could be heard on the front door, followed by the doorbell. Bluebell leapt up with her hackles rising and her nose pointed towards the closed door.

They all looked at each other with misgiving. An ominous knock on the front door, on a Friday evening with a thunderstorm at full pelt never boded well. Low voices could be heard, followed by a shocked gasp. A few footsteps were heard approaching the door of the *hive* which was cautiously opened and Antonio's head appeared, looking around to see if his children were all present.

He cleared his throat, 'erm ... can you all come into the lounge to talk to the policeman please? Now!' ... he added as there was no movement from the playroom. They all seemed frozen in shock.

'Why, Dad?' Bud came to his senses first. 'What's happened?'

'It's important. Come now please ... all of you.'

They walked slowly, in trepidation of what they would find in the lounge, but were met by a friendly local policeman brushing raindrops off his coat. A young, community police lady was also with him, sitting quietly on the settee.

'Hello you three, we are just going around all the houses in the locality asking if anyone has seen anything suspicious this evening.' Bud, Blip and Batty all started to relax. Then the policeman took out his tablet for reference purposes and made a statement which made their hearts almost stop. 'We are looking for a ...Michael and Wayne Wilton, who both live opposite you, we believe. They have both gone missing,' he added seriously.

The police lady said, 'They haven't been seen since the end of school today so we are just trying to ask a few questions to see if we can find out who spoke to them, or saw them, last.'

Batty gasped quietly to herself, but luckily, not loud enough to be noticed. She looked in anguish at Bud and Blip, trying to attract their attention.

'Have you three seen them anywhere ... they are usually somewhere around?' Antonia asked.

'We saw them just before tea, at the end of the road.' Blip spoke up, 'but then we all ran home because of the storm. That must have been before 5.00 I think.'

'Did you actually see them go home?' The policeman asked Blip while inputting the details.

Bud answered for him. 'No sir, we were all in a rush to get undercover and my sister was still a bit upset as she had been involved in calling for an ambulance for old Mrs. Smythe.'

"O" and "A" looked at each other. 'You didn't tell us Gina,' said Antonio in surprise.

'Too many other things were happening at teatime, Dad.' Bud helped his sister out again.

Batty glanced gratefully at her protective elder brother but still managed to ask in an anguished voice, 'So were we the last ones' to see Mickey and Wayne, Sir?'

'I don't know yet m'dear; we have only just started to visit the local area. I suppose the boys are both friends of yours ...?'

Batty looked even more horrified.

'...But there's nothing to get worked up about at the moment, so don't worry.' The policeman continued ... 'They will probably show up later on.' He started to get up and move to the door. 'We'll come back if we need to ask any further questions, if that's ok Mr. Santorini?'

'Yes, that's fine, officer.' Antonio nodded his head quickly and escorted the two visitors to the door.

Returning to the lounge, Antonio found his wife making her peace with Batty and asked in more detail what had happened with Mrs. Smythe. When they heard the full story they both gave her a big hug. They were very proud of their independent daughter, even after the upset over the phone and her hair, but when the whereabouts of Mickey and Wayne were also discussed, Batty started to squirm and pulled meaningful faces at Bud and Blip.

It took them some time to catch on, but eventually Bud said, 'Can we go back to the *hive* until bedtime Mum? We were having a "B" meeting tonight.'

'No problem,' their Mum smiled at the reference to the meeting. 'I'll bring you some supper in an hour or so. Don't worry too much about Mickey and Wayne, they'll soon be found. They've probably wandered off somewhere, knowing those two delinquents.'

Bluebell scampered quickly after Batty, afraid of missing out on something, while Bud and Blip ambled slowly behind. The two boys exchanged glances and then looked meaningfully towards their sister. They were ushered into the room and the door was deliberately shut behind

them by Batty. They all resumed their places sitting cross-legged around
the chest.

Batty couldn't sit still and was looking more and more distressed –
particularly as the boys were starting to smile and treat the whole thing in
a more light-hearted manner. They pushed and shoved each other around a
little until Batty slapped the top of the chest really hard! She had always
seemed older than her years and had often wanted to slap some common
sense into her brothers ... even though they were both quite a lot bigger.

'Stop it you morons.' She glanced heavenward in frustration. 'We are in
deep trouble, haven't you realised yet? For God's sake – why am I the only
one who can add two and two together?'

'Oh come on Batty, it's time to ease up and start to work out what we
can really do with this *fantastic* opportunity.' Blip held his hands wide apart
and then indicated the chest in front of him.

Batty also held her hands wide apart but then indicated bashing their
two heads together! When she had eventually calmed down and found
enough patience to speak, she spoke slowly and emphasised every word.
'Blip *wished* for Mickey and Wayne to go *far* away.' She paused
melodramatically ... 'THREE times!'

She let it sink in.

Blip laughed nervously. 'No I didn't, I didn't!' He denied it ... and then
hesitated as he started to remember. Bud just looked on in horror.

Batty listed the wishes... 'One – when we were pushing the chest on the
sledge.'

Blip thought back and then nodded slowly in agreement.

'Two – when we were waiting for the bus on Thursday.'

Blip's nod was almost imperceptible.

'Three – just before we ran in from the thunderstorm earlier tonight.'

Blip covered his eyes in despair.

'Oh... my... God! Where the hell is *far away*?' Bud added a few more uncouth yet pertinent comments aimed at Blip.

'I can just wish them back again; three times ... it's easy.' Blip stated hopefully.

'You've forgotten that we seem to get punished for wishes that aren't *good* ... so how is it going to be easy?' Bud was almost white with anger. He rose to his feet in frustration and at that moment a huge flash of light momentarily lit up the entire playroom.

Bud froze.

He was facing the playroom while the others on the far side of the chest were facing the door. Bud seemed to have stopped in mid-breath and it took a few seconds for Blip and Batty, who were in mid-argument about the pros and cons of making further wishes – to eventually realise that Bud was acting strangely. They grew still and Blip turned his head very slowly to see what Bud was staring at. Batty froze and just kept staring at the chest. She didn't want to know why they were both staring and why their mouths were gaping open. Strangely, Bluebell was quite calm and relaxed, even quivering her tail slightly.

The vivid flash of light had suddenly lit up the room for a split second and Bud had detected a slight movement out of the corner of his eye. He found himself studying a pair of eyes gazing back at him from behind a set of bookshelves which divided the room. They were startlingly clear, piercing, grey eyes. Bud gulped.

A slim, lithe youth gracefully materialised from behind the bookcase. 'You will have to fetch them back.'

CHAPTER SEVEN

'**Y**ou will have to fetch them back.' The gentle, smooth and fluid voice, quietly instructed the three of them.

Batty turned slowly, nervous... unsure – but wanting to see the person behind the silken voice. Bud remembered to swallow and Blip eventually closed his mouth. Bluebell gave a small 'phuff' of welcome.

The youth seemed a few years older than Bud, but not as lanky. He was graceful and elegant, casually dressed in a loose, white shirt with light grey jeans. But there, the unremarkable and ordinary ceased and the extraordinary began. His ivory-white wavy hair had isolated, shiny threads running through it and his distinctive eyes seemed to flash with a steely fire.

Bud found his voice and stuttered 'W–who, who *are* you?' He wasn't really expecting an answer and he wondered whether to shout for his Dad to go and fetch the police back.

'I am Uriel – I come with the chest.'

Bud abruptly changed his mind about getting the police and he sat back down with a bump. Uriel joined them, his graceful movements seeming to glide over the carpet and he gently placed himself beside Batty. Bluebell moved out of the way to allow him to sit, but then put her head on his knee and looked adoringly at him as if she had known the unexpected visitor for years. For some reason they couldn't easily explain – the children all felt quite contented in his presence ... perhaps sensing the power emanating from him.

'Why are you here? Who are you? Can you help us?' Batty smiled tremulously.

'If you knock – I will answer, if you ask – I will bestow
I'll be there when you entreat me and all darkness overthrow'

Blip looked puzzled. 'We might have made wishes ... but we didn't knock.'

Uriel stretched one hand forth and slapped the top of the chest as Bud and Batty had both done on separate occasions. 'You knocked.'

'You are with the chest?' asked Bud, wanting corroboration. 'It was you who granted the wishes?' The fair youth nodded slightly.

'Can you help us put things right?' asked Batty, still worried about how they might be punished. Uriel nodded slightly again.

'Ok! All this seems to be my fault,' admitted Blip regretfully. 'If I ask, three times, for Mickey and Wayne to be returned ... will it be granted?'

'But you shouldn't have asked for such a wish in the first place,' interrupted Bud.

'Exactly!' the decisive comment came from Uriel. 'If you make such wishes ... you have to take responsibility for the consequences.

Ask for what is 'just' without the pain, heartache conveys
Ask for greed or longing – and torment the end of all your days.'

Blip winced and pulled a face.

'Ok then,' Uriel grinned at him, 'enough of the poetry... but you do need to fetch the boys back; they cannot find the way on their own. They do not have the means to return.'

'Where are they?' asked Bud. 'Why can't they get back themselves?'

'Far from here, a long, long way. They are on the beautiful, yet sometimes sinister, island of Thelasay. It is a parallel world to this, so they do not know *how* to return. This rescue is yours to fulfil, as you caused the problem ... but beyond that, I cannot see clearly as Thelasay has been blurred in my mind.' He paused. 'For that reason I cannot go myself.'

'Then how can we fetch them, Uriel?' asked Batty. '*We* can't go to a parallel world!'

Uriel hesitated. 'You remember how you got your new phone?'

'I'd rather forget it,' Batty didn't like being reminded.

'How *did* you get it?' asked Blip curiously.

'I put my old one in the chest, made my three wishes and then opened the chest,' Batty said quickly, not really wanting to recall the experience.

'Wow,' stated Blip open-mouthed.

'The new smartphone was in the same corner of the chest as the goldfish. I couldn't believe my eyes – I nearly screamed when I saw it,' said Batty still uncomfortable with the thought of what she had done.

'Material goods do not rectify any problems you may have,' Uriel said, but not unkindly. 'You have to face them ... not hide behind something else.'

'I'm sorry Uriel. I should have known that I have to deal with it myself.' Batty looked a little downcast.

'So ...' said Blip, not enjoying the sermonising as he later put it. He wanted to bring the subject back to the question of how they were going to get to wherever Mickey and Wayne were trapped. 'How *do* we fetch them back?'

'It is your responsibility Blip – so you will do the same as Batty did,' instructed Uriel. 'Only, you won't need any wishes, I will send you on your way.'

'What do you mean?' asked Bud suddenly getting involved. 'Send him on his way... in the chest?' Bud was disbelieving and shocked. 'You can't do that!

'Then how will the boys return? It is Blip's responsibility ... it was *his* wish.'

'Is the chest a p-portal? Wow!' Blip stroked the chest as if it was a pet dog, but Bluebell whined softly at him. 'It's ok Bluebell, it's only a wooden chest.'

'It is more than just a chest Blip ... as you will soon discover if you accept your responsibilities.'

Bud thought carefully. 'Uriel – *who* are you? You arrive in our playroom; appear out of thin air, spouting poetry ... and then you want to send my younger brother to another world?' Bud looked intently at Uriel's face, meeting the stranger's piercing eyes with his own puzzled frown. After a few moments looking deeply into those clear eyes, he felt himself relaxing. Bud nodded his head, sighed and gave a rueful smile. 'Who are you ... do I know you?' he looked puzzled as he seemed to recognise the youth from somewhere. He shook his head slightly as he couldn't remember where. 'More importantly... do we trust you?' he continued.

'I cannot tell you my role, *now is not the time* – but you *can* trust me if you can find the strength to do so. I come with the chest and I have granted your wishes. But, you do need to be aware of what your wishes can do and so choose more wisely from now on.'

Bud took a deep breath. 'Ok, I am the eldest,' he said ... 'I will go with Blip ... he mustn't go on his own.' Bud had made his decision.

'I'm coming too.' Batty was petrified but didn't want to be left behind.

'You are not – you will stay here with Bluebell.' Bud was adamant. 'When do we have to go, Uriel?'

Uriel rose abruptly to his feet, without any warning and stepped back behind the bookshelves. 'Finalise your plans for tomorrow morning. I will be here to show you.'

'Here's your supper!' said Antonia as she burst through the door blinking with the sudden, blinding flash of light. All the children were gazing wonderingly around the room but she didn't notice. 'What a night,' she said, looking out of the darkened window. 'The lightning seems to be getting worse.' She balanced the tray with the food and drink on top of the chest. 'You have thirty minutes and then Batty needs to go to bed.'

'Oh Mum!' whined Batty and then changed the tone of her voice as she noticed the small crusty rolls filled with thick rashers of juicy bacon. 'Oh thanks Mum!'

Bluebell barked her thanks and then sat up staring fixedly... and expectantly ... at the plate on top of the chest. Bud and Blip grabbed their bacon rolls before Bluebell's slobbery tongue could claim what she thought was her tea – even though she had completely cleaned her bowl out earlier.

'This is an unusual chest!' "A" suddenly noticed the massive item taking up a large portion of the playroom. 'Where on earth did you find it?'

'On the beach,' said Blip indistinctly, his mouth full of food. The three looked at each other warily, expecting further questions, but Antonia accepted his brief explanation and seemed to lose interest.

'Ok ... thirty minutes remember, Batty.'

'Ok Mum.' Batty agreed quickly, so as not to delay her Mum from leaving the room, in case she suddenly decided to show more curiosity. The three glanced warily at each other and then carefully scanned the room ... but their secret visitor had gone.

'W-who-who was that?' said Batty sounding like a confused owl.

'Oh my God ... fetch Mickey and Wayne back. How ... where ...why?' asked Blip in confusion.

'I will go, wherever it is.' Bud was worried but felt responsible as the eldest.

'Woof,' said Bluebell ... but she just wanted the last bacon roll.

Batty shared part of her roll and Bluebell painstakingly licked her lips over and over again, in order to extract every lingering trace of bacon fat.

The three siblings all sat for a while gazing into the middle distance with unfocused eyes and then gradually, hesitantly, began to make plans for the next day. Later they all went to bed, mentally exhausted and completely overwhelmed by the days' proceedings.

* * *

The Friday night thunderstorm had cleared the air and Saturday dawned with clear skies and a fresh coastal breeze. The three Santorini's were all up bright and early, to the surprise of their father who looked over the top of his newspaper and lowered his reading glasses pretending he couldn't believe his eyes. 'Is something happening today that we don't know about?' he asked perceptively.

'No Dad, we've just got a games contest on the go at the moment – some of it is online so we need the computer in the playroom.' Blip spoke so quickly he almost fell over his words. 'It's going to be really good. We have already signed up Stu and Sandy. Some of Bud's friends said they would join us online, Cousin Marco too, it – it's going to take most of the day we think; b–but it might not. Is that ok?'

Bud and Batty had looked at him in admiration at first, but they soon started to get fidgety when his story looked as if it was becoming unravelled. Antonio shook his head in resignation. He had only understood that they were all going to be in the playroom, and therefore out of his way for most of the day.

Mum appeared at the kitchen door while they were still munching their breakfast. 'Dad and I have to go out this morning and we'll probably not be back for lunch, so I am making you some sandwiches and snacks now. I will leave them covered up on the kitchen table. Don't make a mess! Bud... you're in charge – we'll be back late in the afternoon.'

'Ok Mum. I will keep them under the thumb and make sure they both wash their little hands properly!' Bud teased them.

'Oh no you won't!' chorused Blip and Batty.

Batty added ... 'We'll make sure Blip's hands are clean. You never know *where* they have been,' she grimaced.

'Ricki ... You will make sure you do as Bud says ...' came the comment from the kitchen.

'Ok, but I'm not doing what *Batty* says. She's younger.' Blip was adamant as he pulled a face.

'But cleaner!' Batty often managed to have the last word.

With their parents safely out of the house, Bud and Blip collected the small amount of belongings they had each packed in a small rucksack. They hadn't a clue what to expect so they had tried to pack a few useful items for the day including their lunch. 'You will just have to cover for us Batty ... we will be back as soon as we can,' Bud advised. Batty's lunch was left in the kitchen but she surreptitiously managed to place it under her jacket ... which also shrouded a small bag.

They opened the playroom door in trepidation as to what they would find ... but Bluebell scampered in without any fuss and greeted a patiently waiting Uriel with an excited yelp. Uriel smiled at the three youngsters (who had all heaved a sigh of relief) and softly stroked Bluebell's head.

He looked searchingly at their faces and said gently ... 'I said I would be here.'

'We weren't sure if we had all dreamt it – it is so fantastic,' Bud admitted.

'Are you ready? There is no time to waste.'

Bud and Blip nodded. 'What do we do?' asked Blip.

'I will explain, but firstly let me say that you will need to find overnight shelter.'

'Overnight!' said Bud, 'but we can't. We need to be back.'

'You *will* be back. It is likely to take you a number of days in *Thelasay* but only a matter of hours here. You will need shelter and you will need to keep safe. It is not a risk-free environment.' Uriel held their attention with his own clear grey eyes. 'Don't be afraid to ask for help, but be careful whom you trust.' Bud and Blip nodded seriously.

'Where will we find Mickey and Wayne?' asked Bud.

'What sort of place is it anyway?' Blip wanted some details.

'I cannot answer your questions; I can only see a dark smoky mist in my mind at the moment. It is a beautiful island as I have said ... but quite a large island so the boys could be some distance away. Come, it is time to go.'

Uriel led them to the chest and opened the heavy lid. 'It has been so designed that you cannot close the lid completely with someone inside. This 'catch' is deliberately too big to allow space for you inside the chest in its present position. So it has to be swung out like this ... and then it holds the lid slightly ajar. It means you cannot get trapped inside.' Uriel showed them the turning mechanism.

'What about the key? Wouldn't that lock the chest?' Blip wondered.

'There is no key. *I am the key,*' stated Uriel with finality.

'OK, I'm first,' said Bud, 'but I don't think I can fit my legs in there.'

'You could always leave them dangling outside,' said Blip helpfully ... 'like a giant spider.'

Uriel smiled. 'You *can* fit in – but you will need to fold your knees up.'

Bud twisted the catch over the edge of the chest as he had been shown, in order to give himself enough room and then slowly lowered himself inside. Blip handed him his rucksack which he tucked under his knees and then he bent forward with some difficulty, so that Uriel could close the chest lid.

'Hold on!' called Bud as the lid started to close. 'What do I do? What do I say?'

'Nothing ... hold tight!' said Uriel – not very reassuringly.

Bud could just about see around the inside of the chest due to the crack of light from the lid but he couldn't see anything to hang on to. He was about to call out again, when there was a click as Uriel lowered the lid onto the catch, followed by a sudden flash of light.

In the playroom Blip and Batty just noticed the flash of light seeming to come from the inside of the chest and then Uriel pushed back the heavy lid. The chest was empty. Blip and Batty both gasped and Bluebell barked loudly.

'Do not worry – all is fine, he will be waiting for you Blip. Come.'

Blip approached the chest with some trepidation and placed his small rucksack in one corner. He climbed in carefully, the catch already being in the correct place. Blip was a lot smaller than Bud and he thought he might rattle around, so he felt around the chest with rather shaky hands. He asked nervously ... 'what do I hold on to?'

'Your rucksack,' smiled Uriel.

Bluebell tried to climb inside and Batty had to haul her away. The catch clicked into place before Blip could ask anything further and once again there was a quick flash from the inside of the chest.

Batty was left alone with Uriel who looked enquiringly at her. She recovered her jacket and bag from where she had hidden it behind the door; took a deep breath and said, 'My turn.'

'Are you sure?' Uriel looked keenly at the anxious girl.

'I'll be more frightened if I sit here waiting.'

'Then you need to go soon, but I have something extra for you to take with you ... if you agree. There is no pressure – just a request as I, myself, cannot *openly* return to Thelasay at the moment.' Uriel took a small, shabby leather-bound book from his back pocket. He opened it and taking out a folded piece of parchment, he placed it in Batty's hands. 'If you all agree to the quest, you would be looking for a treasure ... the clues are on this parchment.'

'The treasure from the chest?' asked Batty excitedly.

'Not exactly... but something beyond value, so keep the clues safe,' he said referring to the parchment. 'It is an important quest; the item was stolen from me and must be returned in order to safeguard Thelasay and its population.'

'How was it stolen Uriel? How could anyone steal from you?'

'I was tricked and held "spellbound" for a while. My mind and thoughts were cloaked and shrouded with inky blackness and I was overcome.' Uriel shook his head as if trying to clear it. 'Some of the blackness is still with me and that is why I have to ask others' to fulfil the quest ... but I can only *ask.*' He reassured Batty. 'It has to be your group decision and not forced upon you all. You must talk to Bud and Blip and decide if you are resolved to accept the challenge.'

'And if we don't?'

Uriel smiled at her and gently touched her hand. 'Don't worry – that is for me to find a way.'

Batty placed the parchment in the front section of her bag and then indicated that she was ready to go. Uriel opened the chest again and checked that she could climb in easily.

'We will be back soon won't we? Otherwise Mum will get worried ... particularly now that Mickey and Wayne have disappeared.'

'It should only be a few hours ... don't worry.'

'Bluebell – stay here – Stay!' she instructed sternly. Bluebell immediately sat down beside Uriel, staring at the chest with her sad, brown eyes.

Uriel was about to shut the lid, but just before he did so, he spoke quietly ... 'I will be there in your darkest hour. Look for me. Listen for me.'

Just as the lid was lowered, Bluebell launched herself into the chest, refusing to be left behind. The lid clicked and there was a bright flash. Batty's mind whirled dizzily, for a few seconds, as she held on tightly to a warm and very comforting dog.

CHAPTER EIGHT

A gentle fizzing of waves could be heard as Bud slowly unfolded his legs and climbed out of the chest looking warily around. He assumed that he might need to be careful for a few minutes while he got his bearings, and waited for a slight dizziness to dissipate. He could smell the sea and hear a few seabirds calling raucously to each other. Bud quickly scanned the beach and thought he could see a small inlet in the distance, where a small river joined the sea. Then he heard a brief grunting sound from the chest as Blip struggled to throw open the heavy lid.

'Hey – are you ok?' Bud offered a hand, but his head was on a swivel, busily looking around the bay.

'Oooh ... I think so ... my head feels a bit fuzzy.'

'It's just a bit of dizziness. It will pass in a minute,' Bud advised.

Blip climbed out of the chest with a bit of help and they both sat nearby, searching in their backpacks for one of their drinks. Blip looked around him in surprise. 'Great cove,' he said. 'It would make a cool holiday beach.'

'It would totally ruin it,' said Bud scathingly. 'Listen to how peaceful and quiet it is.'

'Shall we shout? If Mickey and Wayne are nearby they might hear us,' Blip suggested.

'No. Let's wait until we have explored the area … just in case.'

'Just in case of what?' Blip warily glanced around the sand dunes.

'Just in case,' repeated Bud. 'Let's be careful, it's better to be safe than sorry.'

Bud decided to reach for his knife from the front of the rucksack, but as his hand started to unfasten the strap, he froze in alarm. Blip had also stiffened after hearing a slight whimper and rustle from nearby. He could feel his pulse-rate quickening and he deliberately took a measured step backwards so that Bud was in front of him.

'Stay here,' whispered Bud as he crawled up the nearest sand dune so that he could peep over the crest and remain partly hidden by some coarse marram grass. There was a short pause followed by an angry altercation but Blip sighed with relief as he heard Bud's indignant comment. 'Batty – for God's sake what the hell are you doing here … oh my God - *and* Bluebell?' Bud announced in shocked disbelief.

The boys both scrambled over the sand dune and immediately recoiled as Batty was sick all over Bud's large feet and Bluebell ecstatically welcomed them by racing around in circles, yelping excitedly and scattering sand everywhere.

'Oh gross,' remarked Blip referring to Bud's feet. 'She always does that when she's been on a roller-coaster,' he reminded Bud.

'I haven't been on a roller-coaster,' remarked Batty, immediately feeling better now that she felt less dizzy. 'Ooh sorry Bud … do you want a hanky?'

Bud picked up one foot at a time and shook them tentatively. 'Not Blip's hanky, I've got enough muck on my feet already … and shut that dog up,' he added.

'You're not using my hanky to wipe those feet thank you very much.'

'It wouldn't make any difference,' said Batty sarcastically. Blip glared at her.

'Stay here both of you - while I go and wash my trainers in the sea ... My *new* trainers,' Bud sighed heavily. 'I'll talk to you when I get back,' he warned Batty.

They both sniggered as they watched Bud making his faltering way down to the sea – rather like a drunken penguin with a verruca on each foot. Bluebell decided that they must be going wave-chasing (which she adored) and raced down to the shoreline after Bud.

Batty soon recovered completely and had a small drink while they both waited for the castaways to return. On her suggestion they replaced the catch and completely closed the heavy lid of the chest so it wouldn't be full of sand by the time they needed to return home. They also laid some heavy clods of marram grass over it so as to camouflage it. Blip stuck a large, thick stick vertically into the ground and placed two large stones rather suggestively around the base so that they could recognise the place again.

Batty eyed them and gave a resigned sigh. 'Whatever happened to 'X marks the spot'?'

'Boring!' quipped Blip.

Bud returned looking a little cleaner and more refreshed. His grin and comment of 'oh cool!' when he saw Blips *signpost* made Batty lift her eyes heavenward, but as he seemed to have forgotten his warning about dealing with her, she stayed quiet and went to fetch a bedraggled dog back from the tempting waves.

When Batty returned, Bluebell's long pink tongue was hanging sideways out of her mouth as she lay down, panting uncontrollably.

'I think we should be careful with the drinks Blip – if we find fresh water we must make sure to keep the bottles filled. We will need extra for Batty and Bluebell now too!' Bud sighed.

'I've got my own drinks ... and I didn't intend that Bluebell should come, she just jumped into the chest on top of me!'

'Well if you had stayed behind as I told you – Bluebell would have stayed with you.' Bud was angry and didn't bother to disguise it, but Batty wasn't fooled and knew it was because he was worried. She stayed silent and didn't react.

They had each packed two drinks, their lunch and a few extra food items for later. Both boys had also packed a small knife as they had no idea how they would be able to supplement their food rations if they were indeed here for a few days. Uriel had hinted that there were people around even if some were not to be trusted and Bud's ultimate hope was to find the "trusted" folk. He also thought that Mickey and Wayne would surely have tried to find someone to help them.

'Right – let's take stock and plan,' Bud took control. They all sat down together. Blip and Batty were waiting for Bud to make the initial decisions, yet were not afraid to make their own opinions known, if needed.

'We need to take care of any water and food.' Bud counted on his fingers. 'We need to find a safe shelter while we reconnoitre the area and try to find some help – which will hopefully lead us to *those pair*,' he said scathingly. 'We also need to make sure we remember where this beach is. This is our way home. We don't really know just how big this island is... or even *where* it is,' he added thoughtfully.

'I suggest...' he continued, 'that we go towards what seems to be a smallish river and then move inland a bit using the river as a guide.' He pointed towards the inlet. 'There should be some clean, fresh water available and if there are any villages around, they may be situated near a river anyway. There are still plenty of trees around in case we have to improvise a shelter.'

Blip and Batty both nodded their heads in agreement.

'We'd better get started' said Bud decisively.

All three of them rolled their jeans up in case they had to go paddling. Their trainers would cope with the wet as they were often thrown into the washing machine and had to dry quickly. They tied their jackets around their waists and slipped their bags over their shoulders so as to keep both hands free. Bud was a little worried that they only had lightweight waterproof jackets with them, in case the weather turned a lot colder at night. He shrugged his shoulders – there was nothing they could do about it now.

They set off over the fine white sandy beach, keeping an eye open for any signs of human habitation, but saw nothing. Bluebell ran ahead, always checking behind to see if they were following – and then she was off again, ready for a new adventure.

The cove was surrounded by a tall forest which rose steeply beyond some small dunes, blocking their view of the surrounding area. However, when they reached the inlet, they discovered it was a small pebble-strewn river flowing into the sea with what looked like a stony path running along one side. Bluebell immediately splashed about in the water enjoying a refreshing drink.

'This looks more positive. Let's try down here for a short time and then have some lunch. Perhaps we can climb a tree and see what is ahead?' Bud looked doubtfully up at the trunks of the trees rising vertically from the forest floor.

'I'm hungry now,' said Batty wondering what the time was.

Blip suddenly had a brainwave. He pulled his ever-present phone out, in order to check the time for Batty 'Hey, I know, let's see if our phones can tell us where we are with the GPS tracking,' Blip shielded the screen of his phone in the bright sunlight, but Bud interrupted.

'I've tried – there is no signal and none of the apps seem to be working either.'

Blip sighed, 'sorry Batty ... let's keep going for half an hour or so and then we can eat,' he tried to reassure her and caught Bud's eye meaningfully.

Bud understood Blip's warning glance and nodded in agreement. 'Ok ... let's just see what's around that bend in the river,' he pointed up ahead.

They started walking purposefully along the uneven, stony path, Bud and Bluebell leading – then Batty, with Blip bringing up the rear. They were used to walking trips with their parents and had also been camping a few times, but Bud started to feel a little more relieved as the characteristically straight conifers gradually changed to more deciduous-type trees with many forked branches and wide bushy leaves. These were better suited to building emergency shelters.

Their path took them near some blackberries growing in the nearby undergrowth and they halted briefly to eat a few and to gently fill loose pockets, in order to take some with them. Bluebell spat one out in disgust so Batty reached for one of the small biscuits she had put in her bag as an afterthought. Bluebell happily crunched this and then looked for more.

They continued their trek and as they reached the bend in the river, the path noticeably widened and they were able to look a little further ahead. Bud, being the tallest, thought he could see the land rising through the trees and some steeper hills in the distance, but the tree canopy still obscured most of the view. They sat on a fallen tree stump beside the river and pulled out their lunch.

'I suggest we only have half of our lunch and the blackberries, in case we need something for later.' Bud was still in control but was feeling more and more nervous now that he had Batty and Bluebell to look after too.

'The blackberries won't last too long without getting squished anyway,' observed Batty.

'Bud, let's finish one of our drinks and fill the bottle with water here, in case we can't get any later.' Blip looked at the river bubbling over rocks and pebbles. It looked clear and unpolluted. Bluebell thought so anyway.

'Ok,' said Bud, 'but we keep it for emergencies. Did you say you had brought two drinks Batty?' asked Bud suddenly.

Batty smiled triumphantly, 'I brought my lunch, two drinks, some biscuits and all the oranges I could find, but they are heavy so I don't want to lug them around for hours on end!'

'Oh good, we'll have them later,' decided Bud.

They slowly ate part of their lunch – a couple of filled rolls (which they shared with Bluebell) and the inevitable boiled egg which was a family requisite for picnics. Blip commented … 'Mum must have realised we would be eating out,' he sniggered, 'but it seems funny to be peeling a hard-boiled egg in the middle of an unknown forest.'

'What shall we do with the rubbish?' Batty asked pointedly as, out of the corner of her eye, she caught sight of Blip throwing his egg shell away.

'Oh come on Batty – leave it out,' Blip sighed.

'No she is right. Let's dig a small hole for the egg shell, but we'll take the foil and the plastic bags with us, they may come in handy for something.' Bud looked around still feeling a little uncomfortable about their situation.

They cleared up and tried to dig a hole for the rubbish – which was made more difficult by the presence of Bluebell who thought it was just another game and tried to dig it all up again. They carefully filled their bottles with the crystal clear water and continued their way along the path, still with some trepidation as to what was ahead. Blip went first this time and Bud brought up the rear, occasionally looking backwards over his shoulder as he tried to shrug off the feeling that they were being followed. He hadn't heard anything – it was just an uncomfortable prickling of the hairs on the nape of his neck.

They continued in this way for a couple of hours, only stopping briefly for a drink. As the sun started to dip lower in the sky and there was a complete absence of signs of any nearby village or human habitation, Bud started to make plans.

'Hey you two ... I don't know just how quickly the sun goes down here, but it is likely to get dark quickly amongst these trees. I think we need to look for a place to make a temporary shelter. We can eat later.'

Bluebell was also starting to look a little weary and was just trotting by their side – she hadn't been on such a long walk for many months. They continued for a short way, keeping their eyes open for anywhere that might offer some shelter. Bud was now feeling the responsibility of being the oldest and was starting to get really worried. Blip, in front, was still treating it like an adventure and was eagerly looking out for an available "den". His head was almost on a swivel as he looked from side to side.

'Bud – what about over there?' he pointed to the right of the path slightly away from the babbling river. There were some ferns overhanging a large boulder near a short, but steep incline of the forest floor. Nearby was a large beech tree with many conveniently forked branches.

'Perfect,' Bud smiled in relief.

The three of them cleared a small area close to the boulder. Bud and Blip went to strip some large branches while Batty collected ferns and bracken and some short branches with bushy leaves. This was hard going with just a couple of small knives and by the time they had collected some suitable greenery and a few strong branches and sticks, the sun was just going down, making the area more difficult to see clearly. Bluebell half-heartedly chased a few small sticks, but was then quite happy to lie down and just wait for them.

They did their best, stretching their main branch from the tree to the top of the boulder – using the boulder as the back of their shelter. They then tried to lean some other branches onto this main frame and covered the sticks with all the greenery and bush material. It wasn't perfect and Blip announced that a stiff breeze was probably going to blow it all over anyway.

'We are away from the coast now, so the breeze has dipped. Hopefully it won't rain, but it will give us some basic temporary shelter.' Bud tried to reassure them both as Batty was starting to look a bit apprehensive.

'Let's place our waterproofs on the floor so we can sit on something dry and then eat the rest of our food.' Blip could be quite sensible when required and they all cheered up with the thought of having something to eat.

They sat outside the shelter on convenient boulders and logs while they quickly ate the rest of their food – sharing as much as they could with Bluebell. It wasn't enough, but it helped. Batty pulled three oranges out of her bag and they got really sticky as they devoured the juicy segments. They all stumbled to the river to rinse their hands, but by now it was really dark and they could hardly see. Bluebell helped by barking a few times whenever she thought she was being left alone.

They quickly sought the false security of their shelter with Batty and Blip crawling in first and settling down with their backs close to the boulder and with a warm dog between them. Bluebell fell fast asleep with her legs quivering occasionally as she chased imaginary rabbits. Blip and Batty smiled and settled down deriving some comfort from their proximity to such a relaxed dog.

Bud pulled a torch from his bag and laid it close to hand. Then he crawled into the entrance of their bushy tent-like structure and he sat gazing out into the darkness for a time, his long legs stretching out in front of him.

'Bud, why don't you put your torch on for a bit until we get off to sleep?' Blip suggested.

'I'm trying to save the batteries and the moon is about to appear from behind that cloud. We'll be able to see a little more, then,' Bud said hopefully.

'I've got my torch too,' Blip reminded him.

'I know. Keep it safe for the moment. I suggest you two try and get some sleep as soon as you can. I'll stay up for a while.' Bud tried to reassure the others – but he was really wide awake and fidgety and knew he wouldn't be able to relax.

The moon drifted slowly through the clouds, sometimes causing a slight luminescence to glow over the river and at other times plunging the whole area into a stygian blackness. Bud dozed off occasionally but kept jerking awake as he heard the hoot of a questing owl and every impulsive bark of a solitary fox.

A few hours later, he warily opened one eye at a time as the hairs on his neck tingled and he felt his flesh crawl as he suddenly shivered with an uncontrollable fear.

CHAPTER NINE

A putrid abhorrent smell – like rotting, decaying flesh assailed his nostrils. Bud nearly gagged with the overpowering stench and his senses heightened to screaming point as he peered into the almost total dark. His ears felt as though they were primed and ready to catch even the slightest sound. He held his breath ... and his hand gradually moved to his belt to grasp his rather pathetic knife.

He gazed warily at the hazy moon, realising with an inward trepidation that it wasn't a cloud obscuring the steely-grey sphere, but a shadow – rather like swirls of black smoke, growing in intensity until the moon was totally obscured. Bud found himself staring into the keening darkness trying to glimpse any movement in the trees.

His ears caught a soft, sibilant hiss in the air near his face – and he shivered as he caught a foul waft of putrid breath, threatening to overcome his senses. The dark smoke, the complete and utter sense of evil and foreboding was filling him with uncontrollable panic. He was petrified as to the thought of what was approaching the ramshackle shelter and felt totally inadequate when it came to how he could protect himself and his siblings.

The sensation of evil and harm was slowly growing stronger and closer and Bud became aware of a more frightening, threatening quality to the sensations. He stared and stared, trying to see beyond the darkness and eventually thought he could perceive an indistinct, shadowy figure, almost indiscernible due to the smoky quality which kept shifting and rippling out of shape. Bud could sense that it was slowly advancing and he felt an impending doom approaching. His heart was beating painfully in his chest and adrenaline suddenly surged, triggering an absolute panic.

He switched his torch on and off really quickly hoping to pinpoint the problem and then instantly leapt shakily to his feet, gasping and whimpering in fear... 'No! No, oh please... please – No! ... Blip – help me someone!' Bud yelped and gulped ... and almost blindly launched his knife with as much ferocity as he could muster. He aimed it at the centre of the billowing shadows he had detected, as they wafted and converged on the perimeter of the shelter. Momentarily, he glanced behind him as he heard Blip and Batty suddenly stirring.

Bluebell, for some reason was lying awake, but was being very still and quiet. She shook her head a few times as if she had something caught in her ear and gave a few whimpers.

'Wha-What's happening' Blip called sleepily and then quickly realised that something was very wrong. He scrambled to his feet and launched himself to the entrance to stand by his elder brother who was trembling with anticipation of impending doom.

'Batty ... stay there! Hang on to Bluebell!' Bud had heard Batty struggling to her feet.

'Ooh no-o ... Bud ... what is it?' Blip's voice broke in fear, 'p-pass me my knife Batty ... now!'

Batty fumbled in Blip's rucksack and grasped the knife in her hand ... but just as she attempted to hand it to Blip, she heard both boys cry out in terror. She swiftly hid her face in Bluebell's fur, as a rippling, dark shadow scudded from the forest.

Immediately, a huge, resplendent spark of flame crackled and momentarily lit up the small copse with a radiant light. Bud and Blip both ducked spontaneously as the menacing shadow shrieked raucously as it swooped straight for them. It suddenly veered offline, to skim right over their heads, ruffling Bud's hair with the speed and fury of its passing. They both fell to their knees and gagged as the foul smell threatened to suffocate them.

Slowly ... gradually ... the smell and stench of evil lifted, to be replaced by a warm, calmer and more comforting gentle breeze which stirred their hair and cooled their sweat as they gradually picked themselves up and looked all around. Batty and Bluebell joined them at the entrance.

'What was it?' she asked, still sobbing with fear. The boys were speechless – they couldn't answer and just stood gazing out towards the river. The clouds had gone and the waxing moonlight shimmered on the river, highlighting its luminescence. All three of them heard a gentle brush of wings and what sounded like a dull thudding of hooves fading away into the distance. Bluebell gave a rather forlorn whine of relief.

'What in the hell's name was that?' Blip's voice came out as a squeak and he cleared his throat. 'Bud, are you ok?'

Bud was breathing heavily and his eyes looked tortured in the moonlight. 'I'm still here ... I think. Blip, Batty, it's all right now ... it's gone.' He tried to reassure Batty and comforted Bluebell by stroking the soft fur on her head, although his hand was still shaking.

'How do you know?' wailed Batty.

'Can't you feel the change? Everything feels calm and reassuring now, as though the night has been refreshed.' Bud could be quite lyrical at times.

'Was that hoof beats we could hear... over there?' Blip waved generally further upstream.

'I think so,' said Bud.

'What flapped its wings ... was it an owl?' Batty was starting to recover.

'I heard one hunting earlier,' Bud hesitated.

'Well it was a bloody great big owl then,' Blip announced.

They stood still for a while their eyes constantly searching the dark, until they finally started to relax. 'Come on folks, I think we need to rest. We don't know what we are going to find tomorrow yet. I'll keep watch while you two get some more sleep.' Bud ushered them back into the shelter and made sure they bedded down again. 'Keep a hold of Bluebell too – she's a bit upset, I think.' Bluebell whined softly as she heard her name mentioned.

'Wake me in a couple of hours, Bud. Then you can get some sleep too.' Blip yawned in spite of the earlier panic. He was feeling quite reassured and relaxed now, the air felt warm and gentle somehow.

The rest of the night passed uneventfully, but slowly. Bud woke his brother as the dark started to lift in the early hours of the morning. Blip decided to keep himself awake by making himself useful and he started to look for Bud's knife in the undergrowth. He eventually found it – with the blade discoloured and even blunter than it had been previously. Blip tried to clean it on a small hillock of grass and then went to pick some more blackberries he had seen earlier.

* * *

The sun rose, shyly peeping through the branches and numerous birds decided to celebrate the promise of light and warmth with a resonant chorus. Batty and Bud roused themselves to a small breakfast of fruit and biscuits. Bluebell had already gone foraging in the forest and had refreshed herself with some icy cold water from the stream. But she hadn't gone too far ... she was still feeling a little insecure.

The blackberries were supplied by Blip, and the last two oranges and biscuits were supplied by Batty who shared the food out between them –

with Bluebell getting an extra ration of biscuits. Bud was still looking tired and troubled and ate sparingly.

After a slight rest, they packed their belongings, left the shelter as it was and resumed their journey into the unknown; pausing only briefly to rinse their hands and fill their water bottles.

The morning passed slowly. They were all tired and stressed and were unsure where the path was leading them. Bud tried climbing a tree after rounding yet another bend in the river but was unable to see too far ahead – apart from the peaks of some rocky hills in the distance and what looked like a ruined tower perched on a high cliff.

He scrambled back down, picked up his discarded rucksack, and they all continued forward as there was no other alternative at this point. Bud however, secretly decided that if they couldn't find some signs of life today … or Mickey and Wayne, (he didn't count them as signs of life), then they would return to the cove as quickly as they could travel.

They stopped briefly, late morning, as the only food items they had available were half a packet of biscuits left over from breakfast and a handful of sticky sweets found in Batty's pocket. However… soon after resuming their weary journey Bud stopped still and smelled the air. He signalled to the others to be quiet.

'I can smell smoke, wood smoke – like a bonfire. Let's be careful. Shh … and keep Bluebell quiet!'

The track led down to the river which looked quite deep in places and was flowing quite rapidly. Bud noticed some stepping stones leading across to the other side where the path continued to wind through the trees.

He pointed at the stones and then signalled to the others that they were going to cross the river – but in silence. Carefully lifting Bluebell and cradling her in his arms (as he didn't want her to do her usual excited splashing routine whenever she saw water), he stepped tentatively onto the flat stones hoping they were secure. Bluebell gave a slight squirm but when he gripped her more tightly and reassured her in a quiet voice, she just licked his nose encouragingly. Blip and Batty followed closely behind.

When they reached the other side, Bud put Bluebell down but kept a tight hold of her collar until Batty came to one side of him and grasped it with one hand. They stepped off the path into the near forest ... trying to walk quietly and slowly through the trees, parallel to the track they had been following. A few minutes later they thought they could hear voices just ahead and Batty gave Bluebell her signal to stay quiet. Bud signalled them to keep behind him as they moved warily around a large tree. The twisted and tortuous branches provided a form of camouflage for the three youngsters and they drew alongside each other to peep through the bushy leaves.

They found themselves staring at an untidy, but spacious clearing in the forest. It was quite a large area of scrub-land covered with dirty, sandy soil and very little vegetation apart from a few lonely bushes at intermittent intervals. There were a number of dilapidated huts covered with a rough thatch and a few scrawny hens pecking at the dusty ground. At the centre of the small village was a crackling, spitting, wood-fuelled fire with a spire of white smoke rising from it. A youth was sitting cross-legged beside the fire, poking it sullenly with a large stick. His clothes, which looked vaguely familiar, were dirty and torn and his greasy hair was tousled and standing on end. He suddenly gave the fire a bad-tempered whack causing bright sparks to scatter around the clearing.

'Mickey!' yelled Blip and dodging Bud's outstretched warning hand, he leapt through the trees and into the open space. Mickey looked up in disbelief and froze into immobility as Blip approached the fire and gazed down at the confused and bewildered boy. A few villagers drifted out of their huts to see what was happening and Bud decided the time for secrecy was over. He walked slowly into the clearing, with Batty holding onto Bluebell's collar, trying not to cause any further alarm.

Mickey couldn't believe his eyes as he recognised Blip and swore violently. He slowly got to his feet, noticed Bud and Batty also approaching and to their consternation he burst into sobs. Loud, traumatic sobs that shook his body and left him choked.

Blip caught his arm in a tense greeting, 'Mickey! Where's Wayne? ... Are you both ok?'

'What... what are you doing here? Blip – Bud – have you come to rescue us? We need help ... now!' Mickey collapsed into the dirt and covered his face with his hands. 'Oh God, we don't even know how we got here. What did we do? I want to go home Bud!' His voice broke again and he started to tremble.

'We have come to try and take you home ... but it may be difficult.' Bud didn't want to promise anything; he wasn't sure how they were all going to get back to the beach. A few villagers slowly and uncertainly started to appear from the huts and from the fringes of the forest.

'Are you ok?' Blip asked again, tentatively eyeing Mickey's battered school uniform with misgiving.

'Mickey, where is Wayne?' asked Batty. She had been watching the approaching villagers with trepidation but was more disturbed by the absence of Wayne.

'He's... he's ill... r-really ill – oh God,' Mickey stammered in agitation. 'They found us wandering in the forest and have been looking after him for two days now.' He indicated the two young villagers who had cautiously walked right up to the campfire and had just sat down beside him.

Bud indicated to his troubled siblings that they should also sit down and he gazed curiously at the olive-skinned and brown-eyed youths who, likewise, were warily watching Bud. There was a boy, a bit older than Bud, perhaps about sixteen or seventeen and a girl who looked younger, around Batty's age. They both had long, untidy black hair and wore what seemed to be loose, home-spun, sack-cloth type clothes.

Bud wondered how they were going to communicate and was just about to start gesticulating with his hands when Blip interrupted his thoughts. 'I'm Blip,' he said simply. 'This is Bud and Batty,' he indicated the others.

Bud was about to make a sarcastic comment to Blip under his breath, when the boy replied.

'Kall,' he indicated himself, 'Sula,' he pointed to the girl.

'You understand us?' Bud was astonished.

'Quite well,' commented Kall. 'We were taught ... Pastor Kiran ... before he died,' he added sadly.

Mickey sat sullenly and silently, staring at the fire whilst the others traded information as to what had happened over the last two days. An older man with prematurely white hair, who had been watching carefully, nodded to himself in acceptance of the developing situation and stepped back into a nearby hut.

'Where are we?' asked Bud curiously, 'the village... the island?'

'We are in the village of Mowl which is in the north of the Island of Thelasay,' said Kall simply. He was about to give more information when Sula interrupted.

'Mowl means bald,' she said indicating the almost bare clearing. 'This is our hut.' She indicated the nearest dilapidated wooden shack. 'Our home,' she said simply.

'Where are you from?' asked Kall. 'Are you looking for these two boys?' He added ... 'The forest is not a place for lonely strangers; even local people can be led astray.'

Bud started his description of their journey through the forest – without giving anything away about how they got to the beach in the first place. When he got to their experiences of the previous night, Kall and Sula nodded in understanding, but then looked warily at each other and suddenly grew tense. Their hands went up, as if to ward off any threat.

'It got that close to you?' Kall asked in consternation.

'It went straight over our heads,' Blip boasted. 'We ducked.'

'But we all heard wings and hoof beats. Is that all part of it?' asked Batty.

Kall and Sula exchanged glances again, only this time they sighed with relief and smiled in awe. 'You were protected' stated Kall simply.

Blip was just about to ask for further details when Mickey interrupted. 'Oh come on you lot,' he said. 'What about Wayne, can you help or not?' then he added selfishly, 'I want to go home … now.'

'You said he was really ill,' said Bud. 'What's the matter with him? Where is he?'

Sula answered, 'Mickey and Wayne met the same problem as you – only they had no protection.'

'We were attacked … monster … black … smoke. It got Wayne. Infected him – Oh my God get me out of this place!' Mickey slobbered and gabbled almost incoherently over some very strong memories.

Kall continued calmly, 'Mickey here seems to have passed out with fright, (Mickey spat with venom into the fire) and when he came to; Wayne was in a bad way. He is here in our hut… but we fear there is nothing we can do.'

'What do you mean – nothing you can do?' Blip suddenly realised in alarm, 'You mean… you mean… he is going to die?' Blip was horrified. 'Oh no… is this all my fault?'

'Your fault? Why?' Mickey was immediately suspicious. 'What are you doing here? How did you know where we were? Get me out of here now!'

Bud immediately stopped any further conversation and looking distressed and anxious, asked to see Wayne. The five of them walked worriedly towards one of the nearest huts – except Mickey who just sat feeling sorry for himself. Blip and Batty stared back at him in disgust. Bluebell gave a low warning growl.

'Hey you,' yelled Blip. 'Stir your stumps and come and help or I'll knock yer bails off with a cricket bat!' He threatened.

'And I'll take out the middle stump!' Batty added under her breath.

Bud and Blip both blinked in mock horror at Batty's comment and hid their grins as they entered the hut. 'And we are not leaving without

Wayne.' Bud's voice promised the morose and peevish boy left alone by the fire.

The hut was dark and smelled a little damp and moist, but not unpleasantly so. As their eyes became accustomed to the gloom they started to pick out various shapes; three piles of what looked like dried moss and ferns, covered with crude blankets, an assortment of bowls and pots, and a shabby workbench and loom with a few wooden stools scattered around. The white-haired man they had noticed earlier was sitting near the workbench and another figure lay huddled on one of the blankets.

Kall indicated the man, 'Our father, Jalen. He won't understand everything you say.' They all nodded acknowledgement to Jalen who briefly nodded in return.

'Here is Wayne.' Sula moved to the huddled figure. 'It is not catching, but he is very ill. He has succumbed to the dark plague.' Sula shook her head sadly as the others gasped.

'The plague?' gasped Blip.

'It is known as the Subyx plague. It is borne by the smoky, keening shadows – the 'wraith' you experienced last night.' Kall explained ... his voice breaking. 'It is why our village is nearly empty, it is why Pastor Kiran died and it is why our father looks like an old man. He is the only survivor of a recent manifestation.'

'How did he manage to survive?' asked Bud as he glanced at the man who he could now see was only in his middle age and not old age as his hair suggested.

'I... was protected... the white shadow.' Jalen said haltingly.

'The white shadow?' asked Blip curiously, with a rising excitement.

Kall's eyes took on a luminous quality and he started to intone the words to a long-remembered portion of verse.

He comes with the dawn – a white shadow
Stealthily drifting through silent trees
The vision flutters, the mirage fades
A faint brush of wings is heard on the breeze

A black wisp of smoke, a hiss in the dark
The festering stench of demonic fear
The white shadow swiftly soothes the soul
A flash in the darkness at once will appear

He rides against every whisper of evil
With wings to swoop and hooves to slay
The shepherd moves to guard his flock
And protects the very light of day
This — the shield-arm of Thelasay
This — the shield-arm of Thelasay

CHAPTER TEN

*T*his − *the shield-arm of Thelasay...* Batty was entranced and quietly repeated it a number of times.

Bud was listening intently, but Bluebell was too busy sniffing all around the hut.

Blip was pretending to vomit, 'Argh! Poetry again,' but secretly he was really impressed.

'How can you have a *white* shadow?' Bud asked, thinking about the poem '...surely that is a mixed metaphor? And what can it be ... an animal?'

'A unicorn or horse?' asked Batty.

'An eagle?' asked Blip remembering the sound of immense beating wings.

'He is a *"fiery shadow skimming over the waters,"*' recited Kall from some ancient text, which obviously contained even more mixed metaphors.

'And the black smoke?' asked Blip tentatively 'you called it the v−vagous wraith?' He stuttered over the unfamiliar words.

'That is the *dark* shadow... the 'Noctivagous'... it is like looking at the world through a smoky veil. It obscures your normal sight − you can only see and feel the malevolent, evil deeds and thoughts,' Kall continued.

'All I can see is a dirty hovel and a load of brown peasants,' ... a scathing and insulting voice reached them from the entrance to the hut. Mickey strutted through the door. 'What about Wayne? What about getting me home?' He spat in the direction of Kall's feet.

Kall and Sula took a defensive step backwards at the same time that Blip took a flying leap forwards and directed his fist towards Mickey's rather large nose. Bluebell woofed loudly to tell them off, as she always did when there was any arguing. Bud gave a small cheer as Mickey yelled in pain and a trickle of blood started dribbling down his face.

'Make sure you watch your manners you big pig … these good people have rescued and saved you.' Blip was really angry.

'Don't be an uncouth youth,' laughed Bud.

'Ok Bud, don't go all poetical again.' Blip rubbed his fist.

Batty ignored all of them and went to check on Wayne while Mickey retreated back to the campfire muttering, swearing and dabbing at his nose as he did so. He would have stalked off into the forest in a temper … but he didn't dare.

Batty leant over Wayne and wiped his sweating forehead with a wet cloth left nearby. He was muttering and twitching feverishly and his body was twisted with pain. His school blazer lay thrown into a corner but the rest of his clothes were drenched and smelled musty and damp. Batty looked worried. She tried to lift him so he could attempt to drink a few drops of water and Sula rushed to her side to help.

'Thanks,' Batty smiled gratefully at Sula.

'Bud… can we make a wish?' suggested Blip quietly to Bud. 'A wish that he can be healed… I can say it three times?' he said in an effort to convince Bud.

'We are too far from the chest, I think,' whispered Bud.

'Wait!' announced Batty '…is your hanky still dirty, Blip?'

'Oh come on Batty … time to give it a rest now!'

'No. I mean it Blip – is it still dirty?' Batty was insistent.

'Blip, get your hanky out now!' Bud had realised what Batty was trying to do.

Blip muttered and swore as he fumbled in his pocket for his infamous hanky. He eventually swiped it from his pocket and held it up triumphantly; 'The handkerchief! … The handkerchief!' he recited as melodramatically as Othello.

'Very funny,' commented Bud, while Kall and Sula looked on in confusion.

Batty snatched the filthy hanky out of his hand, folded it up into a pad and to Sula's consternation she started to wipe Wayne's forehead with the disgusting article. Bud meanwhile was arguing with Blip about his cleanliness habits.

'I really think you should start wiping your hands on a towel, Blip!'

'Well at least I don't wipe my hands down the side of my trousers!' exclaimed Blip with a scornful look directed towards where Mickey sat outside ... 'or my nose on my sleeve,' he added.

'Well try *washing* your hands first!' Bud grimaced.

'Will you two shush?' Batty continued to wipe Wayne's forehead with the grimy hanky and started to mutter quietly, 'I wish Wayne will get better, I wish Wayne will get better, I wish Wayne will get better.' She paused, 'Oh Uriel, please, please make it work.'

'Ah ... right,' nodded Blip finally understanding what Batty was intending.

Bud, Blip and Batty watched Wayne carefully, almost expecting something to happen instantaneously. Wayne continued to fidget and mutter and he plucked feverishly at the rough blanket. Batty looked worriedly at the others and continued to alternate wiping his face with the hanky and the wet cloth. Bluebell came to help and sniffed lightly at Wayne's face and then gave him a little lick on his clenched hand. Batty smiled slightly as that was the first time Bluebell had greeted Wayne with anything but a growl or a snarl.

Sula moved away to prepare some food and soon they were all gratefully tucking into a meaty stew mopped up with some lukewarm bread. They weren't sure what the slightly *gamey* meat was, but they were all really hungry and swallowed it down quickly – including Bluebell who was given her own bowl. Bud went to take some to Mickey and tried to talk to him about his insulting comments, when Mickey just snatched the bowl out of his hand and starting jamming the food into his mouth as quickly as he could manage. Bud turned away in distaste and returned to the gloomy hut.

Batty and Sula tried to feed Wayne a little of the meat juices and some water while holding his head up, but it just trickled out of his slightly open mouth. They laid his head back down and Batty observed, 'He looks a bit more settled … he is not moving around so much and his breathing sounds a bit better.' She looked hopefully at the others wanting some corroboration.

'I think so,' said Blip doubtfully. 'Can I have my hanky back now?' He was still licking his fingers after the food.

Batty flicked it back at him impatiently and a little of the sandy dust fell onto Wayne's sweaty chest and neck as she did so. She was just about to wipe it off when Bud stopped her.

'No Batty leave it there for a while.'

Sula and Kall looked puzzled but Batty just nodded her head in capitulation. She sat for a while watching Wayne's chest rise and fall. He gradually started to breathe more easily and after an hour or so, he became calmer and more tranquil. A short time later they started to relax as it became obvious that Wayne's fever was actually starting to abate and his eyes were starting to focus.

The evening was approaching and grey clouds scudded across the sky trying to escape from the twilight. Blip and Batty were both starting to feel nervous and looked with trepidation towards the entrance to the hut where they could see the encroaching darkness.

Kall noticed and said, 'you can all stay with us tonight. We will be safe in here and we can make room for you all… but we will have to double up.'

'Blip, will you go and persuade Mickey to come in, he can't stay out there,' stated Bud regretfully.

Blip sighed and went to fetch Mickey, accompanied by Bluebell. 'Hey – Mickey, you need to come in now, we are all going to spend the night in the hut. It will be a bit cosy though cos' we are going to have to sleep together. Wayne's looking better too,' he added.

'I'm not sleeping with any of *them*,' Mickey announced spitefully, ignoring the news about his brother. He moved slightly away from Bluebell who had given a small growl.

Blip waited patiently… but when there was no movement from Mickey, he sighed. 'Ok then you can sleep out here; we'll perhaps see you in the morning. You'd better keep the fire going though, so it doesn't go out… but if you would rather be on your own.....!' Blip gesticulated towards the ominous dark trees, turned his back and walked off laughing. Mickey swore and grumbled, but quickly followed Blip to the hut looking warily over his shoulder at the murky forest.

Bluebell had a good sniff around all the exciting smells around the camp fire, but just as she turned to follow Blip and Mickey, she stopped. Her hackles rose up on the back of her neck and she growled softly as she gazed towards the dark forest. She paused and then straightening her neck she threw back her head and gave a strange, almost unearthly howl.

'Bluebell ... Bluebell ... Come here!' Blip stood in the doorway with Bud and Kall close behind. Bluebell turned and ran back towards the hut. A number of villagers, wrenched outside by the sound of her howl – tutted, then went back inside to secure their doorways.

'Wow ... she's not done that before,' Blip had shivers running up and down his back.

'She did it once, when she heard a police siren and it just triggered her into howling.' Bud remembered.

Kall looked searchingly into the dark forest. 'I think we should all go in. It grows dark.'

They sat around inside the hut and talked for a while exchanging information about their respective lifestyles and the local area which surrounded the village. As the gloom deepened, they all had a little to eat – just some flatbreads and lightly smoked fish followed by a variety of fruits. Mickey turned his nose up at the offering but the others just ignored him. Bluebell offered to eat his share!

Sula prepared a small amount of soup for Wayne who was semi-conscious and propped up a little, but still looking really pale. It was offered to Mickey so that he could feed his own brother, but he steadfastly refused to do so.

'Thanks bro' muttered Wayne weakly, and tried to reach for the bowl himself.

'Let me, Wayne' Batty offered and took the bowl from Sula with a friendly smile.

Wayne looked puzzled and a bit embarrassed, but as he just couldn't manage it himself, he had to rely on Batty's efforts to feed him.

A short while later, the group sat around the perimeter of the hut leaning against the flimsy wooden walls while Jalen placed a section of brushwood in front of the entrance and sat against that.

'We need to plan what we are going to do tomorrow. If Wayne is feeling well enough to travel, then we need to get them both back home.' Bud looked hesitantly at Wayne who could hardly lift his head, but he tried to nod slightly in agreement.

'I'm going back tomorrow anyway. If you won't take me you can tell me where to go,' Mickey said forcefully.

'I'll tell you where to go if you like?' Blip sneered.

'We will all go back together... and as soon as Wayne can manage to walk. No-one will go alone. We will stay together and return home as a group.' Bud stated decisively.

'Then hopefully our quest will be complete,' announced Blip.

Batty gasped.

'*Now* what's the matter with her,' said Mickey nastily.

Batty nearly whimpered in a panic. 'Oh no I forgot... he'll never forgive me. My bag, pass me my bag Blip – now!'

'Oh calm down Batty. Here's your bag ... what's so important?' Blip threw her bag over for her to catch.

'Who'll never forgive you?' asked Bud curiously watching Batty get in a right state.

Batty ripped the front of her bag open and plunged her hand into the pocket. 'Uriel – Uriel. He sent me with a quest for us ... a quest for an important treasure.' She quickly, but carefully, withdrew the piece of parchment from her bag. 'He gave me this; he said it contained clues to find it ... if we decided to try.'

Mickey had looked up at the word treasure and moved a little closer to the others.

'What did he actually say, Batty?' asked Bud as he put his hand out to receive the piece of parchment.

'I *think* he said, 'I have an extra quest for you all and the clues are on the parchment.'' Batty wracked her brains trying to remember the exact words. 'He said we were looking for a treasure... something beyond value.'

'Who is this Uriel?' asked Kall curiously.

'We don't really know – he came with the chest. Oh!' Blip realised he had accidentally let on about the chest.

'The chest?' asked Kall and Mickey at the same time.

Bud realised he would have to explain things in more detail and he started to tell the story – leaving out a few pertinent comments about wishes that he didn't want Mickey to hear. He trusted him even less now he knew him better. Jalen and Sula lit a small oil lamp and a couple of beeswax candles which spluttered and spat, and made the shadows move ominously as Bud continued to explain. As he ended his story, there was a long, quiet pause.

'You said he was fair?' asked Kall, breaking the silence.

'Who is fair ...Uriel? You mean his hair?' asked Bud. 'I think you would say it was white, slightly silvery haired – a bit like your father.'

Jalen suddenly leant forward – understanding more than he could speak. 'Flashes... light... you saw bright flashes?' he asked haltingly.

Bud, Blip and Batty went quiet and slowly looked at each other, remembering the flashes of lightning without any thunder. The bright flashes of sunlight on windows; where there were no windows ... and the brilliant flash of light in the forest last night.

'Why do you ask, Jalen?' asked Bud carefully.

'I was protected,' Jalen explained simply ... 'saw flashes of fire.'

'You think 'our Uriel' is the same as your White Shadow?' asked Blip, almost claiming ownership.

Bud was disbelieving... 'But how can that be? Aren't we from different worlds?'

'Different worlds...' Mickey was horrified. 'How can we get back? I want to go back?'

'You don't mean it do you, Bud?' asked Batty worriedly.

'Is it a different world ... or just a different place in the same world?' asked Kall.

'I'm not sure we are going to find out, not yet anyway.' Bud was thoughtful.

'But Bud...' questioned Blip, 'in our world, treasure chests don't act like time machines or transporters, do they? And yet ours did.' He suddenly laughed, 'Beam me up –Buddy!'

'I know, Blip. I know. I don't understand... perhaps we aren't meant to understand yet.'

'So let's have a look at the clues to the treasure, and let's go and find it,' said Mickey suddenly regenerated with excitement.

'It's not that kind of treasure, Mickey,' Batty attempted to explain again.

'How do you know?' Mickey asked scathingly.

Bud slowly unfolded the parchment. It was very old and fragile and he didn't want to rip it. He looked at it for a second but the candles cast too many shadows and he couldn't read it clearly. 'Pass me my torch, Blip,' asked Bud not wanting to put the parchment down as Mickey had started to crowd him out.

'Here it is Bud,' and Blip passed the torch to Bud, making sure that he elbowed Mickey out of the way as he did so. Bud switched on the torch and carefully read the parchment with Blip hanging on to his shoulder. They both sat back and looked at each other for a moment and then reread it.

'Come on – spill the beans,' said Mickey impatiently. 'Where is the treasure kept?'

'We don't know,' said Bud confused.

'Oh yeah...We really believe that, don't we? So you are going to keep it all to yourselves?' Mickey's mouth was sneering and ugly.

'No, we're not' said Bud 'let's see if *you* can explain it.' He carefully and slowly started to read the clues out loud to the expectant listeners.

Let wise words lead you from the start
To seek the truth of a noble desire;
Pursue this treasure with an unfailing heart,
Be vigilant for that scorching, spark of fire.

To find the pathway within the tower
You must strive to achieve the sight of the blind;
Follow the adit and do not cower,
This shining spirit will ease your mind.

The treasure awaits and lies beneath
The vaulted roof and golden stone;
Lift the supple, guarded sheath
And bring it to this timeless throne.

The chest holds more than just one key
Yet 'night' has seized this mighty gift
She'll pursue your heart – until you're free
When heaven's exalted voice shall lift.

There was silence in the hut while the shadows continued to dance on the uneven walls.

'What the hell is all that supposed to mean?' As usual, the silence was abruptly broken by Mickey's uncouth remarks ... 'absolute codswallop!'

'Codswallop...?' Blip grinned, 'Where did you dig that one up? A bit retro isn't it?'

'What would you know; smarty pants?' Mickey sneered.

'Well he would know if he got walloped by a cod!' Batty sniggered.

'Ok you lot, let's try to work it out sensibly' Bud smiled to himself as he noticed a very confused Kall and Sula trying to keep up with the conversation. 'Kall, we noticed a castle or a tower up on a hill, a long way off ... could that be the tower mentioned in the poem? Is it important?'

'I think you mean the "Linnaeus tower" towards the coast, but it is just a ruin. All that's left is a tower and a couple of walls. I think it was just meant to be a watchtower when it was built so I can't see that it's important at all. There are some game birds around – pheasants and snipe I think, but not much else.'

'Mines ... tunnels under the tower,' Jalen spoke hesitantly.

'Mines... mines... it mentions something about an adit... "*Follow the adit and do not cower*" ... that's a mine shaft surely?' Bud asked those around him.

'What did they mine around here, Kall?' asked Blip.

'Silver, some other minerals, tin, a bit of zinc,' Kall counted on his fingers.

'Silver!' Mickey's eyes shone with undiluted excitement.

Bud sighed, 'It's not that sort of treasure Mickey … as we have said before.'

'And as I have said before … *how do you know?*' Mickey nodded to himself in triumph.

The conversation continued excitedly for some time; many questions being asked, but rarely answered. Eventually, Sula noticed Wayne shuddering in discomfort as he slept fitfully on the makeshift bed. She nudged Batty and indicated the boy twitching, as he tossed and turned trying to find a comfortable position.

'I think we need to stop now, Bud,' Batty spoke quietly.

Bud looked steadily at Wayne. 'Perhaps this is a conversation for morning and daylight … rather than a murky darkness, and spluttering candles casting strange shadows.'

'Let us sleep on it and make our decisions in the morning,' Kall tried to sound confident as he had seen the others glance warily and nervously around the hut.

'I stay here,' Jalen announced and settled down in order to block the entrance of the hut. 'I am protected,' he nodded reassuringly and pulled a rug around his shoulders.

The others still looked uncertain, but as there was nothing they could do, they started to settle down for the night. Batty and Sula squashed themselves onto one bed covered with an old blanket. Bud and Blip settled onto another while Kall volunteered to sleep on the floor near to his father. That left Mickey.

'Oh no,' he shook his head, 'I'm not sleeping on that filthy bed with my diseased brother. I might catch something.'

'He's your brother,' Blip started to get angry again; 'don't you care at all?'

'It's ok Blip – if he doesn't sleep with Wayne he can sleep on the floor!' smirked Bud.

Bluebell settled down near to Batty as she usually found Bud too bony and Blip to fidgety. Batty laid her arm protectively over Bluebell's back and cuddled her closely, both dog and girl deriving comfort from each other. Bluebell laid her head close to Batty's and occasionally licked the tip of her nose during the night. Batty smiled in her sleep.

Mickey disturbed everyone for a long time as he grumbled and groaned, trying to find a comfortable position on the hard floor. Part-way through the night, (an eerie, pitch-black night with many creaks and rustles coming from the roof and the walls), he noticed an extremely large spider scuttling passed his nose and he suddenly and unaccountably, decided to join Wayne, kicking his legs out of the way and poking him with his elbow until Wayne was hanging over the side, partly lying on the cold dried mud.

None of them slept well, they all kept waking and turning over, trying to ease aches and pains ... and listening, always listening, to the night and to the shadows in their minds. Bluebell whimpered quietly in her sleep.

CHAPTER ELEVEN

S mall shafts of sunlight filtered through cracks in the walls. One shaft managed to pierce through the depleted thatch and shone into Blip's sleep-laden eyes as he lay on his side, back to back with his lanky brother. Needless to say Bud's legs were protruding from one end of the home-made bed and his head was poking off the other end making him look rather like an eel trying to fit into a sardine tin.

Blip pushed himself to a sitting position and grimaced at the sight of Mickey, still asleep, slobbering from one side of his gaping mouth. Wayne was hanging off one side of the home-made bed, but was at least breathing deeply and calmly. Blip caught Batty's eye as she slowly awoke and winked at her when she sighed heavily at the sound of Mickey's robust snoring and the sight of a small dribble of slobber hanging out of the side of his mouth. There was a small woof to herald the morning.

'Ugh!' Batty coughed purposefully and loudly and woke everyone up ... except for Mickey who seemed to be oblivious to the rustles and groans that heralded the evidence of communal consciousness throughout the village. Jalen and Kall went out to help the villagers re-light the smouldering fire which had been left to its own devices during the shadowy night. Sula (with Batty's naive help) started to make some flatbreads and a porridge type concoction for an early snack.

Bud and Blip dragged Mickey from his home-made mattress and they all went to wash in the bubbling river, taking Bluebell along. It was icy cold and they all shouted with laughter as the clear water woke them from their slumbers and washed away the fear and discomfort of the night. Bluebell got very excited and soaked everyone as she splashed around. Mickey found himself in harmony with the brothers for the first time and smiled in genuine enjoyment. Kall soon joined them as they paddled and splashed in the shallow water.

Batty meanwhile had tried to wipe Wayne's forehead and face to make him feel better.

'Argh – what – what are you doing?' Wayne woke up and tried to back away from Batty, but didn't have the energy.

'Stop worrying; I'm only washing your face. I'm not going to give you a blanket bath,' she said not very reassuringly, as she was giggling at the time.

Wayne didn't have the energy to respond and lay back looking exhausted. Batty suddenly stopped giggling, noticing his white face and the dark circles under his eyes. She got some water and helped him to drink a little.

'Will you try and eat something this morning Wayne?' she asked kindly. 'I'll help you if you like.'

Wayne opened his eyes slowly to look at Batty and tears started to appear as he realised she was being kind and gentle with him, and that she was actually concerned about him. He realised she wasn't being sarcastic or teasing him, but he wasn't used to people being concerned. Mostly he just got ignored at home. He sniffed.

'It's ok Wayne,' Batty smiled reassuringly this time, rather than giggled. 'You'll feel better soon.'

Wayne tried to grasp Batty's arm. 'Don't leave me alone Batty, I don't want to be left alone – I don't want it to come back,' he shuddered and shivered at the memory.

Bluebell and the boys returned at that point, bursting into the hut looking for something to eat. Wayne turned away in embarrassment while Batty directed the others towards Sula who was busy preparing the food with her father and some other villagers, by the camp fire. The boys all settled around the fire with a few of the villagers and ate a bowl of hot, creamy cereal sprinkled with fruit and spice. They all had a second helping while they discussed their plans for the day and their journey to the tower. Bluebell was given a bone which she had to protect from the scruffy village dogs, but she was used to protecting her bones and none of the other dogs dared to come near her whenever she wrinkled her nose in a snarl.

Sula took some food into the hut for Batty, who had stayed around to reassure Wayne and to make sure he wasn't left alone. They tried to coax him into eating some of the cereal and he managed to swallow a few mouthfuls and then lay back exhausted, again. Batty was worried that he was not continuing to improve and went to talk to the others while Sula sat by the entrance to the hut.

It was soon decided that the four boys would continue with *The Quest* as it was now entitled, and that Batty and Sula would both stay with Wayne in the hope that he would recover enough to be able to move in a day or two. Jalen agreed to stay with the girls once he had returned from a nearby village where he had some business to discuss briefly with a distant relative. It was decided that Bluebell would stay to protect the girls – but really it was because Bud thought she might get in the way of 'the quest.'

So the plans were made; food and drinks were packed into Bud's and Blip's rucksacks and Kall had a canvas bag. Mickey had had nothing on him when he had suddenly appeared on the island, but surprisingly had agreed to help out by carrying a rucksack occasionally. They also packed the piece of parchment containing the clues and their torches. Kall disappeared for a short time before they were due to set off and eventually returned with three sturdy ponies in tow.

'Oh wow!' Batty loved animals and immediately went to stroke their noses.

Kall grinned. 'This is Sage, Guru and Scout.' He pointed to each pony in turn. 'Sage is my pony, Guru is Jalen's pony and Scout is Sula's.' They were various shades of dark brown, and had a shaggy coat, but each one had a different white blaze on their forehead and different sets of white socks. Sage only had one white sock, while Guru and Scout had four. Scout's mane was also light in colour which made him stand out from the others.

Scout

'I will ride Sage, he is used to me. Bud will have to ride Scout – so that means Blip and Mickey will have to ride Guru as he is bigger and stronger.

'Together?' boggled a shocked and reticent Mickey.

'Yes, he is a sturdy pony; he can easily carry the two of you.'

Blip and Mickey warily eyed each other up and then looked with some misgiving, towards a very calm pony munching a mouthful of grass.

'I'm in front – I've ridden before.' Blip announced quickly. Mickey wanted to argue, but as he had never ridden before he thought it might be safer to accept Blip's announcement.

Blip led Guru to a convenient boulder and used it to scramble onto the ponies back, which had been covered with a large padded rug. He settled himself onto a rather indignant pony which then kept turning its head back to see what kind of clumsy creature had kneed him in the abdomen whilst scrambling aboard.

'Move over then,' Mickey announced. 'Make a bit of room for me.' He quickly clambered aboard trying not to show his nervousness and found himself rather too intimately placed behind Blip.

'Ugh – back off Mickey!' Blip was rather put out by the close proximity of his enemy.

'Well stop poking me with those elbows, they are like needles.' Mickey kept trying to push Blip away from his own recoiling body.

Guru, normally a calm and patient pony, had his ears pricked and was moving restlessly from hoof to hoof – but at this point the pony's patience snapped and he bucked suddenly without any warning, and unceremoniously dumped them both on the rather hard, dusty ground.

Bud and Kall laughed with glee and a few villagers came out to watch the fun. Batty just raised her eyes heavenward and went to check on Wayne.

Jalen approached the two boys still lying groaning in the dirt and pulled them to their feet. He led them to Guru and patted his neck reassuringly, showing some concern for his sturdy pony. 'There and there ...' he pointed to where they should sit. 'Keep still ... Guru will lead you.' He handed the coarse rope halter to Blip and gave them both a leg-up onto Guru's back. Neither boy hardly dared to move once they were in position and they started to whisper instructions to each other so as not to upset the unpredictable pony.

'Get your backside out of my way,' Mickey said in a stage whisper.

'Well stop putting your arms around me – what do you think I am – a girl?'

'There's nothing else to hang on to,' complained Mickey.

'Use your knees,' instructed Blip impatiently. 'No – not like that – get them out of my backside! Squeeze them together!'

'My knees – or your backside?' observed Mickey sarcastically.

'You touch my backside and I'll wallop your Cod!' Blip descended into vulgarity, his voice starting to get louder again.

'Well you look really wonderful together, like you're joined at the hip. But I really think you ought to consider how the pony feels and keep still and quiet.' Bud couldn't keep his face straight and turned away to mount Sula's small but well-rounded pony, Scout.

Blip took one look at the vision in front of him and chuckled to himself. Without the use of a modern saddle and stirrups, Bud's dangling legs almost reached down to Scout's knobbly knees and his upper torso towered miles above the pony's small pointed ears and silky mane.

'Hey Bud! You look like you are on one of those pony drawings that Mum loves so much!'

Bud was just about to give a very sarcastic reply when Kall came up to him carrying items that made him look more seriously at his new-found friend.

'We might need extra food – we might need protection.' Kall stated abruptly without any further explanation as he handed Bud and Blip a small dagger each, wrapped in a protective soft cloth. Kall himself carried an unusual, crude cross-bow.

'What about me?' whined Mickey 'Where's mine?'

'Sula has her own knife and I have to leave that with her. We have no more.'

'What about the other villagers ... can't they lend me one?' Mickey asked loudly as he gazed around the clearing, but apart from Jalen and the girls it was now almost deserted.

A dirty, greasy-haired man with untidy, shabby clothes was sitting near the campfire. He turned slowly away and spat contemptuously into the fire which sent angry sparks sizzling and hissing, high into the air. He laughed spitefully at the boys and gesticulated rudely at them, indicating they should leave without hesitation.

'Take no notice,' advised Kall in a low voice. 'That's 'blind Merrick' ... he lives alone in the forest and just appears when he wants something from the village. He can't see you very well anyway – he's blind in one eye and a hawk clawed his other eye when he was younger.'

A grimy, wizened face turned slowly to face the boys and Merrick's light-grey opaque eye could clearly be seen as he sent another shower of greenish spittle in their direction. Mickey suddenly changed his mind about asking to borrow a weapon from him and the boys shuddered slightly as they turned their horses away in order to leave.

Kall, now mounted comfortably on Sage, slipped a small quiver containing a few crude bolt-type arrows, over his shoulder and was just about to set off down a narrow pathway leading away from Mowl village when Jalen called to him. He emerged from the hut, carrying a medium-sized, intricately carved wooden drum with a faded animal skin stretched tightly over the top. He spoke quietly to Kall for a second and Kall nodded in agreement and slung the drum over one side of Sage's back with his cross-bow slung on the other side.

'We'll return soon, Sula,' Kall shouted and then indicated that Guru should follow Sage, with Scout bringing up the rear.

'Keep Bluebell with you Batty, we will be back as soon as we can.' Bud instructed.

Bluebell tried to run after them and was called back by Batty who held onto her collar until the boys had disappeared into the forest. They both watched until the boys were out of sight then turned back to Sula, looking a little forlorn. Bluebell had her tail down and it only gave a little quiver when Batty tried to reassure her.

* * *

The boys travelled in single file for an hour or so, ducking heads to avoid low-slung branches and leaning from side to side as their ponies swerved around large boulders.

'Kall – do you know the pathway well?' inquired Blip after a while, nervously eyeing the uneven, rocky surface ahead of them.

'Sage, Guru and Scout will lead us' stated Kall.

Bud suddenly chortled to himself ...'Ha – the poem, the poem!'

'What do you mean?' Kall was puzzled. Blip was too preoccupied with staying on board Guru to notice Bud's comment and Mickey was almost asleep, his head nodding slightly.

'"*Let wise words lead you from the start,*"' quoted Bud. 'It's the first line of the quest. Sage, Guru and Scout ... they are leading us and they all have names that indicate wise men, or being a leader.'

'Wow Bud – that's a bit deep isn't it?' stated Blip, not liking the smug grin on Bud's face. He was about to make a further comment when Mickey's sleepy head nodded straight into the back of his own. 'Stop bashing my head Mickey!' He sent both bony elbows flying backwards to wake Mickey from his slumbers which succeeded rather too well and Mickey jerked awake so suddenly, he tumbled backwards over Guru's rump and landed in a clump of crunchy, dry leaves. Scout following closely behind, also jerked sideways to avoid Mickey, but it was rather too sudden for even Bud's long legs and he slipped under Scout's belly in a rather ungainly fashion.

Kall sighed loudly and waited for them to dust themselves down and re-mount, while Blip just giggled so uncontrollably that even the placid Guru turned his head around to look inquisitively at the human on his back.

'Oh stop it – Oh stop it – My stomach hurts – I'm going to wet myself.'

'Well I'm not getting back up with you if you've wet yourself,' stated Mickey in horror as he dusted himself off.

Bud stretched his long legs and easily clambered aboard the little fat pony. He ordered Mickey to stop making a fuss or they would leave him behind in the forest. A sharp intake of breath could be heard from Mickey's direction as he remembered his living nightmares that were best forgotten. It all went quiet and even Blip stopped giggling. For some reason they all looked around them with trepidation. The lonely pathway was surrounded on either side by a dark, damp forest and just for a second it had seemed rather enclosed and threatening.

'Let's continue now, while we still have plenty of daylight,' Kall decided for them.

'Yes let's,' agreed Bud. 'Get back on the pony, Mickey – Now!'

'"Pursue this treasure with an unfailing heart, be vigilant for that scorching, spark of fire,"' quoted Blip, taking the idea from Bud. 'I wish we could have that spark of fire now,' he said uneasily eyeing the darkness surrounding them.

'The path widens a bit further on. Let's keep going for a while and then stop for some refreshment.' Kall's advice sounded good and soon they were all back on the pathway again, the ponies picking their way carefully until the path widened and became easier to navigate.

CHAPTER TWELVE

Sula and Batty waved the boys off and then rather nervously watched Jalen disappear in a different direction towards the larger, more central village of Thelasay from which the island got its name. Batty let go of Bluebell who proceeded to snuffle around the village camp fire where someone had earlier dropped some food. The girls, feeling rather bereft and alone, turned their backs on the forest and went to the hut to check on Wayne.

Bluebell had a good scratch around, her ears brushing the dust and her tail wagging vigorously as she found some interesting smelling items, some of which proved to be edible. Her big paws padded around, leaving a few prints in the soft earth. She suddenly stopped and raised her head; her ears twitching as she attempted to recognise the distant sounds. Then with a bound, she pelted off into the forest following the trail that the boys had used.

No-one noticed 'blind Merrick'. He was sitting on the far side of the camp-fire away from most of the huts. His one damaged eye had focused on Bluebell as she made her way around the fire towards him. He was about to stretch his hand out towards her collar, when she had frozen into immobility, with her nose twitching and pointing towards the forest. Then she had taken off after the boys. Merrick scowled; spat into the fire and picking up a large, dirty piece of sackcloth, he shuffled down the narrow path after the dog.

* * *

Wayne was dozing peacefully, so the girls decided to go and wash in the river and then gather some wild fruits and herbs. Sula was going to instruct Batty as to which berries and herbs were edible and which were best avoided, so she picked up a large, rather dilapidated trug and followed Batty through the doorway. She came to an abrupt halt as Batty had stopped in the doorway and was standing stock still, staring around the empty clearing.

'Bluebell ... Bluey ... Come here girl! ... Where are you Bluebell?' Batty's voice started to get more stressed as she called and called – but there was no response. 'Oh no ... Oh please no ...Bluebell ... where are you?'

They rushed over to the campfire ... the last place they had seen her mooching around. Sula looked carefully at the paw prints in the loose earth and then gazed towards the forest with a frown wrinkling her forehead.

Batty followed her line of vision. 'Oh no, she wouldn't ...surely not. Let's check the rest of the village first.' The girls raced around the other huts asking if anyone had seen the dog and where she might have gone. But the few villagers who were around had been inside the huts and had seen nothing.

One older man came out of his hut to look around the village and ominously stated that 'blind Merrick' had also disappeared ... 'Usually stays for any free food – by the fire ... must have gone back to his camp in the forest.'

Batty was blaming herself and getting more frantic. 'What if she gets lost? We have to go home soon. The boys will never forgive me. Oh Bluebell where are you? ... We must go and look for her.'

'We can't go far into the forest, we're not allowed. Jalen will be back later so we will wait ... but don't worry, we won't stop looking for her ... even if you have to return home without her.' Sula tried to reassure.

'But I have to go and look for her, Sula. What must she be feeling if she is lost? She must be getting really upset.' Batty started sobbing and wailing. 'Oh no ... what if that evil smoky-thing gets her? What can I do ... I *have* to go after her!' She looked at the forest trail the boys had taken and took a deep breath.

'Ok ... we can go down the first part of the trail and call her ... she may hear us?' Sula looked at Batty's downcast face and tried to sound hopeful, but she was very wary and suspicious due to Merrick's timely disappearance. The girls checked that a villager would keep an eye on Wayne and then they rushed off down the narrow trail, calling loudly every few seconds.

* * *

Bluebell had raced down the trail, really enjoying her adventure and having a good run. She was still able to smell the ponies' faint scent and barked a couple of times in excitement. She never liked being left behind so she ran quickly in order to catch Bud and Blip as soon as possible. But when the scent started to fade away, she hesitated and slowed right down checking each side of the pathway to try to discover where the boys had gone.

The spaniel started to feel a little uncomfortable and bewildered, as she realised she didn't recognise where she was. Her instinct told her to return to Batty, who she had been with most recently, so she turned – sniffed around a little bit just to check her bearings and then decided to retrace her steps back along the shady path. She set off quite slowly at first and then as she picked up her own scent, she grew more confident and certain she was on the right trail.

Until she scooted round a bend and ran straight into Merrick's open sack!

'Ha got you, you little worm!' *Oh ... She will love you. She wants you ... now...*

Bluebell yelped and growled in panic as it all went dark. She struggled and squirmed as vigorously as she could, making it almost impossible for Merrick to hold her in the sack. He slammed it down roughly and attempted to get a better handhold. A black nose and sharp teeth erupted from the opening in the sack. Bluebell's head appeared ... her nose wrinkling and her teeth displaying in a vicious snarl. She snapped continuously as if her life depended on it. Merrick blinked rapidly and attempted to grab her, but misjudged his aim as Bluebell frantically bit at his hands and managed to free herself from the smelly sack. He launched an aggressive kick as she flew past him, catching her on her hind leg. Bluebell yelped and whimpered as she ran. Ears flapping like wings – she leapt over a fallen tree and escaped into the murky undergrowth.

Merrick swore and spat with rage as he followed the spaniel, knowing his lack of sight would work against him in this suffocating, impenetrable part of the forest. He glanced uncertainly around him. *She likes this oppressive atmosphere ... She could be close ... Is She here?*

The vagrant pulled his soiled cloak around his shoulders and limped into the darkening forest, his head swinging from side to side like a pendulum, his hand bleeding and stinging from the bites he had received. Merrick stared into the undergrowth trying to pinpoint the dog, but with his impaired sight he found it difficult to distinguish any features in the camouflaged shapes. He sniffed the air ... his sense of smell heightened by his lack of sight. He tried snooping around the undergrowth for a few minutes and then hesitated as he felt a shiver creep up his back. He looked furtively around and pulled his cloak more tightly around him.

The atmosphere had changed. The oppressive air had suddenly grown cold and the light had dimmed; the trees seemed to be inching closer together cutting off his path. Merrick knew he could sense *her* disturbing presence and started to back off. He was aware, as her servant, that he was relatively safe from her fanatical desire to feed off any rampant emotions. Yet he was still afraid to be close enough to witness her volatile reactions, which occurred whenever this psychotic hunger had been thwarted. He gave up the attempt to find the frightened dog and retreated to the trail. 'She' would discover the animal herself – or he would find another opportunity to waylay his victim and deliver 'the goods' to her in a terrified and pathetic state.

* * *

Batty and Sula almost ran down the trail, but halted every now and then to call for Bluebell and then stood still, listening for any barks or yelps. The forest grew thicker and darker and it wasn't long before Sula started to hesitate. Batty was still frantic with concern and wanted to continue the search. Sula agreed to go a little further and they walked more slowly – but still called out as loudly as they could. Batty started to cry.

Suddenly they heard a rustling and grunting from the forest itself.

'Bluebell … Bluebell … here girl … here …' Batty yelled again, more in hope than conviction.

They both screamed and leapt backwards as Merrick's dirty, greasy face suddenly appeared between the trees. He struggled over a small bank and then leant forward, bending his spittle covered mouth towards them. He was so close that they could smell his foul breath and he taunted and sneered at them showing his blackened teeth. 'Lost something?' he sniggered.

Batty and Sula backed away – afraid to answer.

Merrick approached them again; his damaged, opaque eyes squinting as he tried to focus on their startled faces. *'She wants her. She wants to feed from her.'* He whispered harshly at the two frightened girls as he shoved past them and limped away up the stony path. His mocking laugh echoed through the trees. The girls watched him go and then sat down for a moment as they tried to decide what to do next.

'What does he mean; _She_ … wants her?' Batty clenched her fists in anguish.

Sula hesitated before she answered. 'I think _She_ … is the dark, smoky shadow … the wraith … which attacked you the night you camped out in the forest. Merrick has always been evil and cruel. *He* works out in the open … whereas … *She* hides in the shadows.'

Batty remembered everything about that night – and wished she didn't. She glanced around her as the forest suddenly became still and felt very heavy and oppressive. The sun went behind some very dark grey clouds and the girls both shivered. A few tears dropped onto the damp earth and Sula held onto Batty as she wept in fear.

* * *

Bluebell also shivered. She was looking very forlorn and feeling sorry for herself as she limped from tree to tree hoping to find the path back to the village. Her back leg was really hurting where she had been kicked and she was only setting it down very gingerly. Thorns and leaves clung to her long, drooping ears. She whimpered quietly to herself and looked around very warily, expecting the cruel, aggressive man to jump out at her again. Where were the children? Why didn't they come for her?

She stopped still and listened. She had heard or felt something in the air. The trees closed in and it grew even darker and more eerie. Bluebell sought the shelter of some branches under a tree and painfully lay down. Slowly … almost imperceptibly … a foul stench wafted through the forest. Tendrils of black smoke twisted and spiralled from the undergrowth. Bluebell trembled and whined softly.

The Nyxx – that blackened, sinister daughter of chaos – sensed the fear and confusion emanating from the dog and gleaned further strength from the anticipation of teasing these emotions into a climax of terror. Her gaping, cavernous mouth opened wider and a wisp of smoke dribbled from her thin lips like a trickle of saliva.

The gruesome feelings of oppression grew more volatile and Bluebell started to panic. Despite her bad leg, she shifted and squirmed in order to escape from the notion that something was starting to creep inside her head and invade her mind. She shook her head, petrified – then suddenly tried to run from her makeshift shelter, but she was pulled up abruptly. Her collar was caught up in the branches ... she was stuck and was going nowhere. Again, she could feel something inside her head and she shook it frantically from side to side trying to dislodge it – but not understanding what it was. It started to hurt as another tendril of smoke hovered in front of her eyes and Bluebell reacted. She instinctively threw back her head and for the second time in this strange world, she emitted the most unearthly, bloodcurdling howl. She did it again; partly to frighten whatever was approaching, and partly to call for help if anyone was close enough to hear her.

Batty was close enough to hear. She wiped her eyes and clutched at Sula. 'Shh – that's her – that's Bluebell!'

'Wait Batty you can't go into the forest ... stick to the path.'

'I *have* to go Sula, can't you understand?' Batty's voice broke, 'I am responsible – I *have* to go for her – no matter what the result. I have to try ... She's in trouble.'

Sula hesitated then nodded. 'Ok, I will come part way into the forest with you, but will stay near the path. You need to try and keep *me* in sight and don't go too far.'

'Ok let's do it – now!' Batty leapt over the bank as she heard Bluebell howl for the third time. She moved as quickly as she could, calling out for her beloved dog every few strides. She kept glancing back at Sula as she made her way towards Bluebell who was now barking frantically in response to Batty's frantic yells.

The Nyxx smirked even more widely as she gorged on that tenacious desire to protect, radiating from Batty, and the trust and unconditional love flowing from the frightened dog. Then suddenly, 'She' was interrupted as the sun burst through the dark clouds, sending vertical shafts of light through the forest. She snarled in anger and frustration and the stench immediately lightened and started to drift away.

Batty looked back once more in order to see where Sula was standing. 'Sula – I have to go a bit further – I think she is just over there but I don't know why she isn't coming to me.'

'Be careful and keep yelling so I know where you are.' Sula took a few more steps into the forest, more confident now that she could see the sun shining on the pathway behind her.

Batty trod carefully around a few trees still calling but now in an encouraging tone. 'C'mon Bluey where are you? Batty's here! ... Bluebell! ... Bluebell! Come here girl.' She suddenly heard her whine nearby and bent down to look underneath some thorny branches.

Two frightened eyes looked out at her and Batty burst out crying as she grabbed her head and stroked her as if she had been lost for years. She realised Bluebell couldn't move and had to yank her collar out of the thorns, scratching her hands badly in the process.

Bluebell went berserk when she was freed from the branches – she was so glad to be back with Batty and she squeaked and whimpered uncontrollably, pawing at Batty's arms.

'It's ok I'm here now, let's get out of here Bluey,' she added as she looked warily around. Batty was really worried when she noticed that she was limping quite badly, but Bluebell was so keen to escape from the forest that she quite happily hobbled alongside Batty. They quickly reached a very relieved Sula, and both girls took it in turns to carry Bluebell back along the trail. When she got too heavy for them, Bluebell made every effort to limp on three legs and in this way they all managed to return safely to Mowl village.

They approached the clearing with a sigh of relief, and were so keen to return to the hut, they had no desire to turn to look back at the forest. If they had ... they would have seen a faint curl of smoke, peevishly twist itself around a shady tree near the edge of the village.

The three wanderers returned to the hut to check on Wayne who was still sleeping peacefully as if nothing had happened. Sula prepared a hot poultice and while Batty made a huge fuss of Bluebell and cuddled her tightly – the poultice was placed on her bruised thigh and then she was given a bone which still had some meat scraps left on it, which Bluebell quickly devoured.

Wayne awoke and when he was told what had happened he bravely held his hand out to Bluebell. He had never been comfortable when close to dogs and Bluebell had snapped at him previously, but now both patients seemed to feel an affinity with one another. Bluebell let Wayne stroke her and then fervently licked his hand. A huge grin lit up Wayne's face ... particularly when Bluebell curled up beside him and fell asleep with her head on his arm.

Wayne stroked her silky ears while she was asleep and pulled a few leaves and thorns out of her fur. He was totally entranced when she grunted softly and snuggled closer to him.

CHAPTER THIRTEEN

They eventually left Bluebell to Wayne's newly discovered attentiveness and went to forage for food as they had originally intended. Batty found a small clump of wild mushrooms under a large tree. She didn't touch them, not knowing if they were poisonous until Sula praised her and said they were all safe to pick and eat. The two girls wandered around the outskirts of Mowl village, gathering blackberries and wild raspberries to add to their collection of mushrooms, cresses and herbs. A few berries found their way into the girls' mouths and they had to return to the stepping stones in the river, to wash their hands.

A scream suddenly split the silence and a panicked voice could be heard babbling away for a few seconds.

Time seemed to freeze – and in that hiatus the atmosphere changed again. The warm, autumn sun became obscured by dark clouds and it grew chill and gloomy. Sula and Batty clutched at each other for support and looked hesitantly over their shoulders towards the village and the shabby hut. A shadowy figure cautiously emerged from the hut and shambled off into the forest.

'Merrick – it's Merrick!' Sula whispered in fear.

'Bluebell … oh not again …and Wayne … Oh my God what has happened? It was Wayne screaming!' Batty was beside herself with her own fear, but mainly with her concern for Bluebell and Wayne. The two girls abruptly set off towards the hut as fast as their courage would take them, shedding a few berries from their basket as they ran.

They appeared in the open doorway to find Wayne, still babbling incoherently with fear, squashed up against one of the walls furthest away from the door. Bluebell, her tail wrapped right under her bum, was quivering and shaking with fear and was trying to push her dry nose underneath Wayne's arm.

'Dark … the dark … it's coming – the black smoke – hissing. Don't leave me alone. Batty don't let it get me!' The final clamour was emitted as a high-pitched wail as Wayne eventually recognised Batty even in his nightmarish premonitions and visions.

'Wayne, it's ok, we're here … it's ok!' Batty tried to reassure him, but was herself, feeling very worried and anxious. Bluebell recognised Batty's voice and threw herself into her arms – scratching and pawing at her in a frantic effort to be as close to Batty's face as she could manage. Batty hugged her closely, 'Oh Bluey I'm here now sweetheart … I won't leave you.' Bluebell whined pitifully and licked Batty's cheek then put her head down and nudged her with her nose.

Sula was busy closing off the entrance to the hut with a section of brushwood and she barricaded it with whatever heavy objects she could find inside the hut. Looking carefully around the hut looking for gaps in the dilapidated walls, she covered a couple of the bigger holes with rugs and pieces of dark cloth while Batty helped Wayne back to the padded bed where he lay wide-eyed, his chest rising and falling as he snatched shallow breaths in his panic and distress. Batty's eyes were standing out like organ-stops as she watched Sula move swiftly around the gloomy hut.

'Sula, what is it?' she asked breathlessly. 'What is happening?'

'Shh, we need to be quiet and still.' Sula whispered to Batty as she tugged her small dagger from under her bedding. She sat down near to Wayne and Batty looking determined.

Bluebell lay curled up as close to the children as she could manage. Batty was scared but resolute and as the light faded, as if heralding an approaching storm; she grabbed her bag and pulled out her torch.

'No torch – no lights – we need to stay hidden in the dark,' warned Sula.

Wayne muttered and whimpered in fear and Batty placed her hand on his arm and squeezed it slightly, trying to comfort him.

'Wayne we need to be silent. We *have* to be silent,' Sula whispered urgently.

Batty held Bluebell's face between her hands and made the trembling dog look her right in the eye. 'Bluey – quiet – Shhh. Keep still now,' she whispered, stroking Bluebell's long ears.

The three children and dog sat huddled together on the mound of bedding, their backs leaning against the far wall of the hut for safety and reassurance. Time passed slowly, the silence only punctuated by rather erratic breathing from all three of youngsters and the occasional soft whine from Bluebell. Batty tried to take her mind off the immediate problem and decided that it was like sitting in her grandma's old creaky house, listening to the grandfather clock ticking loudly in the background.

Except it wasn't the ticking of a clock she could hear, it was a surreptitious tapping on the wooden slats covering the entrance to the hut. She heard Sula gasp slightly and signal to them to remain still and quiet. The already funereal atmosphere grew more toxic and disturbing. Heightened senses approached screaming point, as nightmarish visions started to consume their troubled hearts and minds.

They gradually noticed a foul, putrid stench, seeping through all the small cracks in the walls and thatch. Batty started to gag and heave as the miasmic, noxious odour filled the hut. But it was the incessant, sinister scratching and the glimpse of dark, smoky shapes starting to drift and shift through the air that really triggered the panic.

Wayne started hyperventilating as his distressed breathing became uncontrollable. He gasped and then started to become hysterical and moaned aloud in terror. Sula and Batty tried to shush him and attempted to put their hands over his mouth. Bluebell started to retch and became very agitated. Batty and Sula both put a warning hand on her collar.

Silence.

They stared blindly into the total darkness; a sense of foreboding wafting near their faces, and tendrils of smoke seemed to stroke their foreheads like an evil veil. Batty and Sula whimpered in fright as the blocked entrance suddenly started to shake and tremble violently without warning. Outside the hut, the malevolent wraith renewed its frenzied efforts to reach the physical entities still evading its' clutches. It had already tormented and captured Wayne's mind ... it had reduced the dog to a quivering wreck and fed off its fear, but in order to multiply and gain strength – it needed bodies as well as minds.

The darkness, the terror, was complete. The blocked entrance started to give way under the audacious, determined assault. It was afternoon, but it felt like the stroke of midnight on a savage, tempestuous night.

Sula screamed for her father to save them and come to their aid, which impulsively triggered a blaze of light in Batty's memory. A voice – a soothing, reassuring voice – a sure and certain hope – a light in the darkness.

"I will be there in your darkest hour. Look for me. Listen for me."

'Uriel ... Uriel ...' Batty tried three last desperate pleas and muttered... 'I wish you will save us. I wish you will save us. I wish you will save us.'

The entrance collapsed under the determined assault and crashed to the floor. But at that precise moment there was the most brilliant, startling, burning flash of light that made Batty and Sula hide their eyes in agony. Bluebell was hiding under Batty's arm but Wayne had his eyes covered as he cowered in the corner. The wraith screamed and squealed in pain as if being tortured and the smoky veil was sucked out of the hut and disappeared like a whirlwind.

Slowly ... gradually ... the daylight resumed its usual autumn intensity and a gentle brush of wings could be heard fleetingly in the distance. Bluebell poked her head out from under Batty's rigid arm and gave a small questioning woof.

Batty and Sula gasped and tried to control their stressed breathing as Wayne shakily appeared from under a blanket ... white-faced and wide-eyed.

Sula held her hand up to quieten her friends. 'Shhh – what's that?' she asked in a whisper.

They all froze in fear and their ears strained to catch any sinister sounds.

A soft pounding of hooves grew steadily louder and louder and it seemed as though the dark clouds had instantly disappeared. Bright sunshine beamed through the ruined doorway and lit up the inside of the hut as the three children smiled wistfully at each other, feeling a little embarrassed by their intense reactions. A loud, impatient whinny came from outside the hut. The sound of footsteps in the dust and a glowing face appeared at the destroyed entrance.

A gentle, melodic voice soothed their erratically beating hearts.....

'If you knock - I will answer, if you ask – I will bestow
I'll be there when you entreat me and all darkness overthrow.'

'Uriel!' Batty gave a raucous shriek. He grinned at her while stroking an ecstatic Bluebell who had leapt towards him ... and Batty immediately burst into tears.

'W–who ...? Sula stuttered.

Wayne fainted – but possibly with relief.

A short time later, the three youngsters, now clean and tidy but still a little embarrassed, were seated around the village campfire. Their eyes, at first, were totally focused on the slim, elegant young man sitting opposite, still stroking Bluebell; who wouldn't leave his side. Uriel was still casually dressed in the same light-coloured clothes as before, but in the warm sunshine, his ivory-white hair seemed almost golden. He pulled Bluebell towards him, held her head between his gentle hands and made her look into his clear grey eyes. He spoke to her softly and calmly so that the others couldn't hear. Bluebell quickly relaxed and lay down beside him with her head on his knee, while he gently caressed her bruised leg.

Sula was transfixed with the sight of Uriel. Batty however, couldn't help glancing sideways to where the most beautiful horse she had ever seen grazed patiently on a small mound of oats. Uriel in turn, glanced at Wayne's troubled face ... his eyes still seemed to be glazed and confused and his skin looked pale and clammy.

'It is probably best not to talk about what has just happened, or ask any ultimate questions. Just accept I will be here when you have need of me.' Uriel nodded reassuringly at Wayne.

'I can't ... I don't... Will it...?' Wayne hesitated and stammered over his words.

Uriel stood up and went over to Wayne (followed closely by his limping, devoted fan) and placed one hand comfortingly on his shoulder and the other hand laid gently on Wayne's head.

'I'll be there when you entreat me and all darkness overthrow.'

Wayne's face cleared and he sighed with relief as he gazed up into Uriel's face. 'Who – who are you?' he asked in awe.

'Not yet. Now is not the time.' Uriel shook his head, his hair swirling in the sunlight.

Silence fell between them for a moment until Batty laughed, trying to lighten the atmosphere. 'It's a good job Blip is not here to complain about your poetry again Uriel.'

Uriel smiled, lighting up his whole face, his eyes flashing with fire. He walked around the campfire to his horse. 'I will stop the poetry when Blip returns,' he laughed, 'but come and greet Aisling, my companion on *my* quest.'

Aisling whickered softly as she recognised her name. She was a beautiful, dappled grey horse with an almost white mane and tail. After a pat on the side of her neck from Uriel, Aisling walked slowly up to Batty who had immediately leapt to her feet, in her eagerness to greet the horse. Batty stepped towards her with an almost beatific smile on her face. She gently stroked the velvety soft fur above the horse's top lip as Aisling kept trying to nuzzle Batty's hand.

'She's beautiful Uriel, absolutely beautiful. Where did you find her?' Batty turned to ask Uriel as Sula recovered some of her confidence and went to join Batty.

'She lives here on the island of Thelasay. She finds me when I am in need of her.'

'Is she... Are you...?' began Sula, hesitating to put her question into words.

Uriel vaulted lightly onto Aisling's bare back without answering. 'I must continue my journey – there are others in need of reassurance.'

'You're not going? Can't you stay?' Wayne's panicky voice rose in a crescendo.

'You are safe now.' He turned to Sula, 'your father will soon return and will stay with you all.'

He set off towards the forest trail, but turned to wave and called back to them... 'You will be safe now – don't be afraid.' Then he added, '... But do try to keep away from Merrick. He even managed to trick me!' He smiled and disappeared down the same track the boys had taken earlier that day. There was a pause as the sound of hoof beats faded away.

Bluebell stared after him ...tail wagging and muscles twitching in anticipation. Batty immediately grabbed her collar. 'Not now Bluey – you stay here with me!'

'Let's get something to eat while we wait for father,' suggested Sula.

'Good idea.' The others agreed and went to help her, but not before they had all glanced around to see if any other villagers had returned. The village still seemed deserted, but the sun was now shining and their hearts had been lifted by the presence of Uriel. They returned to the hut to find some food, preparing mushrooms and herbs on a board placed outside the hut and then serving them up with some toasted flatbreads while they sat around the village campfire. The sun was warm and they didn't want to sit in the cool, gloomy atmosphere still pervading the hut.

The villagers slowly returned, including Jalen, and the three youngsters heaved a sigh of relief as he immediately took charge and repaired the hut's detachable doorway, with Wayne's intermittent help. Wayne was recovering well now, but any physical effort soon left him exhausted and needing to sit down for a while in the sun.

As they sat down to rest in the late afternoon, Sula voiced their unspoken thoughts. 'I hope the boys are safe.'

'I do too,' agreed Batty worriedly.

'How far is it to the tower? Will they get there today?' asked Wayne.

Jalen thought for a moment. 'See tower soon ... overnight – then back tomorrow.'

'That's three nights we will have been away from home.' Batty was starting to get concerned. 'I hope Uriel is correct with his timings. He said we would only be gone a few hours.'

'Perhaps three nights here, only means three hours in our world.' Wayne tried to reassure her, meeting her eyes and smiling fondly at her. Batty smiled back a little shyly.

Sula turned away and grinned to herself.

CHAPTER FOURTEEN

Bud stretched his long back and sighed heavily. He was starting to get leg ache and backache as he wasn't used to riding so far ... and also a headache, with all the complaining coming from Mickey and Blip.

'Blip, let me go on the front for a bit ... it's my turn!' complained Mickey.

'No way, you'd ride us over the cliff – you're as blind as a bat and you can't control Guru anyway.'

'... And *you* are controlling Guru?' observed Mickey, watching Blip hanging onto the pony's bushy mane while the halter rope lay dangling near the ground.

'Well at least I'm not wobbling around like a half-set jelly.'

'Well there's nothing to hang onto except your podgy body and I don't want to touch that!'

'I'm not podgy.'

'Yes you are, you still have your puppy fat!'

'Oy you two, shut up or I'll go and fish for that cod to wallop both of you!' Bud had heard enough, 'Kall ... how long now?'

Kall grinned and looked back at the others. 'Nearly there – a couple of miles along the coast.'

'It didn't look this far from the village,' complained Bud.

'We are only walking slowly remember and we also had to go around part of the forest,' replied Kall.

The journey had actually gone fairly well. There had been no emergencies and only one section through the darkened forest where their nerves overcame common sense. They had stopped briefly for some food and refilled their water bottles in a nearby stream while the ponies drank further down. Bud and Blip had shared their spare bottles with Kall and Mickey so that they all had access to some fresh water.

Kall continued to lead them until the path widened enough so they could ride alongside each other. The rather strange watch-tower could also now be seen on a nearby hill overlooking a large rocky bay. They tried moving a little faster and started their ponies trotting – keen to end this part of their journey ... even though Mickey complained about being joggled about and kept saying he felt sick.

After a while they halted in the shadow of the tower, gazing up at it in a rather perplexed fashion.

'The Linnaeus Tower,' Kall introduced them as if it was a being or entity.

'That's a tower? It's a ruin!' Mickey had still not learned any diplomacy.

'It was almost built as a ruin, Mickey – a folly.' Kall explained. 'It was used as a 'lookout' or 'watchtower,' and they also used the site to set up a warning beacon overlooking the bay. According to my father, it houses one of the entrances to the mine.'

The tower consisted of one wall and a large turret which contained a few circular apertures intended as window spaces. At one time it must have had a thatched-type roof – but it was obviously now missing both the roof and a doorway. Their presence had disturbed a few birds from the high walls and as the boys looked up, the sun started to sink lower on the horizon. The fading sunbeams shone through two of the apertures which were almost in alignment. The result was a rather eerie cascade of brilliance, in the shape of an elongated star that seemed to be burning through the tower itself.

Bud stared in awe at the brilliant light and took a deep breath '"*Be vigilant for that scorching, spark of fire*" ... is that what it means – the poem?'

'It's like an oxy-acetylene torch,' Blip stated in amazement. 'I wish my phone was working – I want to take a photo!'

'Let's go and search for the treasure then,' Mickey was impatient, as usual.

'It's not that sort of treasure Mickey,' Bud and Blip chorused together.

I don't think we can do it safely tonight, it's starting to get dark – but let's go and have a look inside the tower anyway,' Kall decided.

They hobbled the ponies near a grassy area and started to climb the rocks up towards the tower. They still carried their rucksacks and bags and Bud and Blip took out their torches as they approached the rather gloomy turret. The sun by now had almost disappeared.

On entering the tower, they looked around them in surprise – it was a completely empty circular space with a dusty, slabbed floor. The blocks of rough-cut stone were enormous and the walls themselves were at least four feet thick. Bud, being the tallest, climbed into one of the window apertures and dragged Blip in behind him. There was easily room for all four of them but Kall and Mickey climbed up into one of the other apertures which faced in a slightly different direction. They looked out across the bay and smiled at the wonderful view.

'Wow, you can see for miles!' Bud remarked in astonishment.

'No wonder it was used as a beacon!' Blip had moved forward in the attempt to see in all directions and nearly fell out of the window space, but Bud just grabbed him in time. Kall was used to the view, having played there with his friends when he was younger, but he derived some pleasure from seeing the exhilarated look on Mickey's face.

Bud had started to look around the circular tower, 'Where is the mine entrance Kall?'

'I'm not sure – it was all closed up for safety when we used to play around here, but the rumour was, that although the main tunnel entrance was somewhere nearby in a copse, there was another secret entrance in here ... actually in the tower.' Kall shook his head, 'We never found it.'

'What does the poem say, Bud?' Mickey asked scathingly, not believing that the poem had helped so far. He preferred to think it was just a coincidence.

'Good idea, Mickey,' said Bud pretending not to notice Mickey's sarcasm.

'Idiot!' Mickey held his hand over his mouth as he pretended to cough.

Bud ignored him and took out the piece of parchment being careful not to damage it as he slowly unfolded it. He read by torchlight...

"*To find the pathway within the tower*
You must strive to achieve the sight of the blind;"

'The sight of the blind ...?' Blip questioned.

'The blind can't see,' commented Mickey scathingly.

Bud thought for a while. 'So what do they do? ...They feel with their fingers when they are reading Braille and that is almost like seeing the words. They are seeing with their hands.'

'Merrick, who is half-blind, always gets close and touches your face to try to feel what you look like,' Kall shuddered with the memory.

'Ok, so let's close our eyes and feel our way around the tower,' Blip thought it was a good idea anyway.

'Well I don't think we need to close our eyes – let's just turn the torches off. They are getting dimmer anyway and we need to save the batteries.' Bud glanced worriedly at his fading torchlight.

'Batty brought some spare batteries with her, Bud. She gave them to me, but there's only enough for one torch.' Blip fumbled in his bag for the batteries.

'Then we will just have to keep together and not get separated, if we will only have one reliable torch,' said Bud, and Kall nodded in agreement.

They switched the torches off and for a second it seemed almost pitch black, but their eyes soon got used to the half-light and they spent some time on hands and knees feeling every slab on the floor and every stone in the wall. Kall was soon ready to give up and suggested that he go and find some shelter and look after the ponies. The others carried on for a while but were soon feeling very dirty and dusty. Blip suggested that they return in the morning.

'Yes, but then we are not searching like a blind man,' Bud pointed out.

'Perhaps you are relying on the quest poem too much Bud?' Blip had been resting in one of the window apertures and quickly slid off as he wanted to go and join Kall. There was a loud 'argh!' followed by a ripping of jeans as he squirmed to the floor and clutched his nether regions.

'What have you done now?' Bud's resigned facial expression said it all.

'He seems to have 'walloped his cod',' Mickey smirked with glee while Blip continued his antics on the floor.

'I caught my trousers on a hook or something... I've split them right down.' Blip was angry as he went to look for the cause of his accident. 'Over here, there's a big hook set in the stones right under the window.'

Bud went to look, but had to use his hands to feel all around for the 'hook.' 'That's not a hook Blip, it's a lever – I think!' Bud hesitated, 'Shall I?'

The others nodded their heads in excitement, but Bud couldn't see them clearly in the ever growing darkness, so he just made up his own mind and pulled. Then he twisted. Then he pushed it to the right.

There was a pause ... then a soft grating sound, as a large section of stones situated under the aperture started to move. The noise stopped. Bud switched his torch on again and they all blinked while their eyes tried to focus. There was a small gap in the wall, just big enough for someone to squeeze into. Blip, being the smallest, moved forward at a nod from Bud and shone his own torch into the hole.

'There's some steps!' he shouted excitedly, 'steep steps going downwards.' His voice echoed down the shaft. 'It smells a bit musty too.'

Mickey also had to push his way forward to have a look, so Bud pushed too, not wanting to be left out.

'Hey folks, watch out – you'll push me down the steps.' Blip pushed back and they all fell back into the main part of the tower.

Bud could see some stars starting to twinkle in the sky above the open roof of the turret. 'I think we had better go down to Kall. We can't do this tonight; this is for tomorrow, as soon as it is light enough.'

They left the shaft open and went rushing down to find Kall. It was now almost dark and they could see a small campfire below the tower. The ponies were safely tethered nearby and Kall had just started to prepare some food, taken from the covered bowl Sula had placed in his bag before they left the village.

'Kall … Kall!' they all shouted as they approached the rough camp he had prepared. They all wanted to be the one to tell him what they had found.

It wasn't long before they were all sitting enjoying a hot concoction of grain with some meat and herbs stirred into it. It wasn't wonderful, but it was hot and the meat was tasty and succulent. They all felt better for the hot food and soon settled down to discuss their discovery while nibbling at some crude chewy biscuits dotted with wild bilberries and a few nuts.

Kall hadn't had time to prepare a proper shelter but they all decided it wasn't going to rain and so they could just use the horse blankets and snuggle down under the nearby bushes.

After clearing everything away, and watering the ponies, they settled down to reread the parchment and to plan for the morning and a very early start. Bud was worried about getting back to Batty and was also impatient to succeed in getting Mickey and Wayne home – hence the early start.

He read out parts of the poem (Blip pulled his anti-poetry face again) and they all chipped in with various comments.

"Follow the adit and do not cower"

'That must mean the mineshaft, surely, but what does 'do not cower' mean?'

'Presumably, don't be afraid? …I think.'

"The treasure awaits and lies beneath
The vaulted roof and golden stone;"

'There's no punctuation at the end of the line so I assume it means that the treasure lies beneath the vaulted roof and golden stone.'

'What is a 'vaulted' roof?'

'I think it is like a church roof, with lots of beams ... perhaps a big space.'

'A 'golden stone' .... Does it mean a piece of gold? ....or a yellow-coloured brick?'

'"Goodbye yellow brick road,"' sang Blip sarcastically and Guru whinnied at the noise. 'Thanks Guru!'

"Lift the supple, guarded sheath"

'Is that the treasure?' Blip asked. 'I don't like that it says it is guarded.'

'Well we will have to deal with that in the morning.' Bud was avoiding the issue, but it wasn't something they could deal with at the present time anyway.

'Try to get some sleep now,' said Kall. 'I will watch for a while.'

'Wake me up part way through the night, Kall,' Bud instructed Kall – and then checked on Blip and Mickey before he settled himself down for the night.

The night passed quickly and calmly and very little disturbed them, apart from the occasional owl hunting for food. Bud took over the watch for a short time, but by the time dawn broke, they were all fast asleep.

* * *

They were rudely awaked by a small flock of young, excitable sheep gambolling into their camp early in the morning. They started bleating at the tops of their voices and although the ponies ignored them, the boys leapt to their feet in alarm.

'Ha, I didn't know sheep could baa in so many different pitches. Listen to that grumpy one over there.' Blip was amused by the deep-pitched bleat of the 'grumpy one' ... a black-faced ewe with curly horns, but was even more amused that Mickey started moaning incessantly about 'blasted sheep' in exactly the same grumpy tone. The nick-name 'grumpy one' was so apt that it soon began to stick.

Mickey however, soon got his own back by referring to the new *vent* in Blip's jeans as often as he could. He managed to refer to an aperture, a hole, an outlet, a drain, and a ventilator in as many minutes. Blip got ready to *vent* his anger and decided he would *ventilate* Mickey's nose – if he didn't shut up immediately.

Bud and Kall called them to order and in a very short space of time they had eaten a small snack, refilled water bottles and packed their few belongings. They watched Kall, deftly entwine some dampened bracken and coarse grass around the end of two sturdy branches to use as flares, in order to save the torch batteries, but they were even more interested in the small, neat tinderbox he carried with him to light campfires.

They checked the ponies and left the rugs in a neat pile ready to grab when needed. Bud also instructed Blip to put the new batteries in his own torch and Bud would keep the old ones' to replace his own rapidly fading batteries at the appropriate time. On a serious note – they checked the daggers Kall had loaned to them, which made Mickey even more moody as he had only been given Bud's small pen-knife.

Kall checked over his unusual cross-bow. 'Home-made,' he said, 'but powerful.' He patted it possessively. They looked all around checking everything was in order and swiftly made their way up to the threateningly, gloomy tower.

The shaft was still open and Kall gasped in astonishment. 'We searched here for years, but we never thought to check the walls. We assumed it would be in the floor area or just outside. The walls are thick enough to be hollowed out to make a passage – but we just never expected it to be here.'

'Neither did Blip's jeans,' laughed Mickey spitefully.

'Ok - ok. Shall I go first as I am the shortest?' the only time Blip admitted his lack of height was when it was to his advantage to do so.

'I'll go second – then Mickey – then Kall. Is that ok?' asked Bud passing his torch to Kall. They all agreed impatiently, so Blip shone his torch into the darkness and stepped onto the top step.

'"*One small step for man – one giant leap for mankind,*"' laughed Blip.

'Oh shut it!' Mickey grumbled.

CHAPTER FIFTEEN

I t was a tight squeeze at first, but once the steps had gone below the level of the walls – the passage widened out slightly and even Bud and Kall could stand almost normally. Kall, being the last in, had very carefully checked that the entrance would stay open and that they wouldn't get trapped, but he noticed an extra-large handle on the inside of the shaft and correctly assumed they could open it from the inside if they had to.

'Good thinking Batman,' smiled Bud, but Kall was mystified by the reference.

'Batman ... Where?' Mickey was starting to get twitchy again.

They ignored him and continued down ... and down ... in a spiral; not bothering to count the steps as they soon started to approach every bend in the hope that it would be the last. It was a long way down and Blip was starting to feel quite disorientated.

'I'd hate to have to climb these in a hurry,' said Mickey without thinking.

'Let's hope we don't have to then,' stated Kall. Mickey drew a quick breath – the darkness and the shifting, sinister shadows caused by the torches were starting to make him nervous.

After what seemed an age, Blip called out. 'Hello – I've come to the bottom ... What the heck!'

'What is it Blip? Let me through.' Bud pushed past him. 'Wow!'

Wow ... ow ... ow, the echoes came whispering back along a dark tunnel. The hair on the back of Bud's neck started to rise as all the boys came to a halt on a wide bottom step and shone the torches all around.

The tunnel stretched in both directions from where they were standing, but astonishingly it had a railway track to one side and some old wagons piled up on the other.

'My dad used to tell me about the old railway track – I think he said it stretched under the sea in one direction and over to Thelasay village in the other. But there was a roof-fall and it became disused when they closed the mine.' Kall stood in awe by one of the wagons. 'They must have carried the ore and tin and all the waste in these wagons.'

'Well the wagons are almost blocking that route ... so I suggest we go *this* way,' said Bud in a decisive mood. He turned towards the tunnel on the left.

'Ok, but please stop talking; I don't like the whispers echoing back.' Mickey looked nervously around and tried to grab the torch.

'Well I don't like the silence – so get used to the echoes,' said Blip grabbing his torch back.

'Hey go easy with that,' Bud warned, 'if we break that one – my torch is not going to last the distance!' Blip and Mickey suddenly stopped struggling over the torch and meekly followed Bud and Kall. It was the start of their underground quest.

They clattered their way down the long tunnel occasionally tripping over the rusty tracks in the dim torchlight. Their plan was to follow the main track for a while and see if it opened out into a larger space anywhere. There was no vaulted ceiling in this part of the tunnel – just dirt and bricks shored up with large pit props. They stopped briefly when Bud's torch gave out, so he could change the batteries and replaced them with the old ones' taken out of Blip's torch.

'These replacement batteries aren't going to last long, Kall. I suggest we give your flares a go for a while.' Bud put his torch safely in his rucksack and indicated to Blip to do the same.

'I'll just wait for the flares to be lit first thank you!' Blip didn't like the dark any more than Mickey but he didn't want to actually say so.

'Ok,' agreed Kall and the boys watched in fascination while Kall slipped out his tinderbox and deftly lit one flare. He waited for it to stop smoking too much and once there was a good flame – he lit the second flare from the first. He gave one flare to Bud and told Blip to turn his torch off.

The restless glow and spluttering flames, cast frightening shadows all along the walls of the tunnel. The smoke threatened to choke them and they all started coughing and clearing their throats. Kall took the lead with Mickey grasping his jacket, while Bud went third with Blip holding on for dear life, to the strap of Bud's rucksack.

They passed a small tunnel going off to the right, but decided to continue with the larger tunnel and railway track which seemed to be heading in the direction of the sea. They walked unsteadily for a few minutes trying not to trip over the rusty railway tracks. Mickey fell once and let out a great yell when he realised he had lost his grip on Kall. They all hesitated while Mickey gathered himself together and then set off again, as they later assumed – under the sea.

After a while, they came to a larger cavern and some crude buffers as the rail track ended abruptly.

'Bud, shine your flare around with me – mine isn't bright enough on its own.' Kall instructed. Bud did as he was requested and they all cheered and slapped each other on the backs as a number of carved pillars and an intricately patterned, arched roof could be seen with the fluctuating light. Two more small tunnels could be seen heading away from the cavern.

'Is that it – is that a vaulted ceiling?' Mickey asked with glee and started to look all around him for the treasure as Bud nodded his head in confirmation.

'The poem says, 'it lies beneath the vaulted roof,' but it also mentions a golden stone – so it must be buried somewhere I would think.' Bud was trying to remember the exact wording.

Time was of the essence so they lost no time in searching the ground for a golden stone; Mickey and Bud following the light of one flare with Blip and Kall squinting in the fading light of the other. The flares were starting to get very smoky and cast more shadow than light so Kall suggested going back to the torches. Blip got his torch out of his pocket while Bud delved into his rucksack where he had safely put his. One bright light and one fading light shone out into the darkness while the two flares were thrown onto a pile of stones to burn themselves out.

They resumed their search and kicked a few old bricks and pieces of rubble out of the way … Nothing. They spent a long time searching around the edges of the cavern … Nothing.

They stopped for a few minutes, turning the main torch off in order to save the batteries and sat on a pile of rubble while they had a drink and discussed their next move. Blip started to pull pieces of stone out of the gap in his ripped trouser leg and threw them over his head in a temper, where they clattered like a small avalanche.

'What in hell's name was that?' Mickey nearly jumped out of his skin and then clutched at Blip while the echoes disturbingly continued to intone his uncouth comments over and over again.

They started to talk quietly and calmly in order to stop too many echoes from resounding around the large cavern – but that meant that faint, disquieting whispers seemed to come at them from all angles. They started to feel uncomfortable, particularly when Kall suddenly held up a hand to shush them. 'What was that?' he said in an undertone.

'*That ... that... that,*' the echoes whispered, ominously.

The boys all fell quiet in order to let the whispers fade away into the darkness. A faint tapping could be heard far away down one of the tunnels, followed by a slight rattle as though someone had accidentally kicked some stones.

'Stop throwing dirt Blip ... please,' requested Bud.

'I'm not! Honest!' Blip was insistent. '*Honest...honest...honest,*' the echoes repeated.

'*Oh hell ...hell ... hell,*' came the next inevitable echo!

'Come on then, last chance ... let's see if we can find this stone and then let's get out of here.' Bud got quietly to his feet and moved to the centre of the cavern right beneath the highest point of the spectacular vaulted ceiling. The others moved forwards with him but they weren't too bothered about finding the stone any more, they just wanted to get out of there.

'Blip, shine the good torch down here please?' asked Bud quietly as he squinted at the dusty surface. Blip did as he was asked, even though his hand was starting to shake nervously. Bud knelt down to wipe his hand over the surface of one dirty slab of stone.

'Keep it still Blip!' Bud was starting to sound impatient so Kall took the torch carefully from Blip and shone it closer to the ground.

'There's something here Kall, look.' Bud wiped his sleeve over the slab and slowly uncovered a few letters carved into the stone. He wiped a bit harder, 'It's a word I think ... an A ...U ... then an R then...' he paused, '...I? Is that the letter I - Kall?'

'Yes I think so Bud – is it a word? ...Or someone's initials?'

Blip was starting to feel the cold and like Mickey, the haunting echoes were making him nervous. 'I don't care if it is anyone's initials Bud, but AU stands for gold so for God's sake hurry up and dig it up.'

'Yes I know, but do you think we need to dig it up or just look nearby?' asked Bud.

By now, Blip knew this bit of poetry off by heart …
"The treasure awaits and lies beneath
The vaulted roof and golden stone;
Lift the supple, guarded sheath
And bring it to this timeless throne."
'So let's do it … quickly,' he added.

Bud hesitated, but Kall pointed out that everything else had followed the clues in the poem and as time was getting short, they needed to do something without wasting any time.

Bud and Kall gave the torches to Mickey and Blip to hold, while they got on their knees and tried to prise the stone up out of the ground with the two daggers they had available. They scraped and dug around the edge and then tried to lever the stone out from the surrounding earth and rock. It was heavy, but seemed to move far more easily than they were expecting. The boys tugged and pulled the stone to one side to reveal a deep black hole. They sat back and looked at each other debating what to do next.

'Come on Bud,' whispered Blip. 'You've got the longest arms – you will have to do it.'

Bud looked thoughtfully and a little warily into the hole. He shone the bright torch into it and realised it was not quite as deep as he had originally thought. He could see that it had been dug out of the rock and shale and that there was a dark, shadowy object lying at the bottom. He handed the torch back to Blip and hesitated before reaching deep into the hole while Kall held onto his legs. It was so deep that his head and one shoulder disappeared into the gloom and a muffled voice could be heard.

'Got it … pull me back out … carefully it's really long.'

Kall started to pull him out and his head appeared like a cork popping out of a bottle. When Bud's lanky arms finally surfaced, they could see in the torchlight that he was holding something long and slender, wrapped in a type of oilcloth.

It was at that point that the smell started to invade their nostrils.

All hell seemed to break loose. Mickey moaned and muttered in horror and then suddenly let out an anguished howl and ran off back into the large tunnel as fast as he could go – taking the fading torch with him. The other three, their eyes wide and frightened, gazed quickly around the cavern and then backed themselves into each other, forming a circle.

'For God's sake keep that torch still, Blip,' hissed Bud. But Blip was panic stricken and he and Bud knew precisely what the smell meant – they had experienced it before on their first night in the forest. Kall could only guess, as his father had described it in detail.

The putrid, sickening smell grew thick and made them gag, trying to catch their breath. A chilling whisper – almost a hiss, grew louder and closer. A feeling of malevolent evil slowly approached the trembling boys. There was nowhere to hide. They had to face this, or run as Mickey had done ... and Mickey had gone quiet after one final, bloodcurdling shriek.

A smoky shadow started to seep into the extremities of the torchlight. Swirling, black, restless shapes slowly moved into the boy's vision and started to billow and grow around the cavern. The torchlight began to fade into blackness. Not that the batteries were giving up – but rather the smoke seemed to be swallowing the light and Bud felt it was like he was looking through dark sunglasses. More whispers could be heard, getting closer – a hissing in the dark, spitting out evil and hatred. The smoke was formless and void at first, but slowly and gradually as all the light faded, they could just discern the chaotic shape of a hideous, menacing female with coal-black eyes – an unearthly queen, ruling the appalling, smoky darkness and presiding over the chaos in their hearts and minds.

Blip, holding his hanky near his mouth, suddenly vomited uncontrollably due to the repellent smell and he dropped the torch which immediately cut out with a slight tinkling of glass. They were plunged into total darkness.

'Down, get down!' Blip heard Bud give a desperate order and the three of them sank to the ground in despair. The daggers and Kall's cross-bow were no use here – you can't stab smoke and you can't kill evil – you have to deal with it in another ways. This was something dark and malevolent and Bud suddenly had a moment of enlightenment and decided they had to fight it with something light and good.

He started to mutter under his breath. Blip tried to catch what he was saying but couldn't hear. 'Hand me your hanky Blip,' Bud broke off from his muttering for a second. Blip was literally petrified, frozen like a stone, so Bud grabbed and scrabbled around in the dirt where he thought the hanky was.

'Ugh thanks Bro!' he commented as his hands landed in something unsavoury. Bud touched a piece of cloth with one hand – grabbed it and resumed his muttering.

The Nyxx – that personification of evil and daughter of chaos, grew closer and closer and Blip fainted away in total fear and dread as he felt soft, icy fingers touching his mind … stroking his face with frigid, icy fingers … tugging at his thoughts, bewitching him to give way.

Kall had hidden his face in his rough jacket and was panting uncontrollably and hyperventilating as he repeated, 'the plague – the plague – the Subyx plague!'

Bud's muttering was growing louder and more desperate as he felt the stygian darkness closing in and he became light-headed and confused. He suddenly felt a huge searing pain in his head as the nightmarish apparition took control of his mind and he screamed out loud in his agony. 'You can't have it – no – get away! NO! Help me!' He started to stutter …. 'I wish ….I wish ….I w-wi…!' Bud shrieked and collapsed with the pain and horror of the *thing* taking over his mind, but he was still grasping the filthy, stained hanky.

An excruciating flash of brilliant light and power lit up the cavern. The smoky veil was immediately sucked out like an inky whirlwind and the Nyxx – that evil queen of darkness and of the horrors of the night – scuttled down a narrow tunnel with a scream like a banshee. The nightmare was pursued by a magnificent, silent creature, strongly beating its' majestic wings and brushing the tunnel entrance with shining, iridescent feathers.

The cavern became suffused with a calming radiance from the narrow tunnel entrance and also in the distance, a very faint glow of a dim torch beam from the main tunnel. Bud carefully shook his head to clear it.

'What on earth was that?' he asked the world in general.

'Bud! I heard wings again Bud!' Blip was just regaining consciousness.

'I did too,' Bud agreed while looking apprehensively all around.

'Let's go now ... while we can!' Kall appeared from under his jacket listening carefully to the complete silence. It seemed that even the echoes had stopped and the mine had become both quiet and calm. Blip was still a bit shaky and Bud helped him to his feet.

Kall started to take charge as if he understood more of what was happening and was recovering from his fright more rapidly than the others. He slung his cross-bow over his shoulder and then felt around for the daggers and the torch. The torch wouldn't work even when Kall shook it gently – the bulb had been shattered when it was dropped. Kall suggested that Blip take the batteries out and stow them away safely. Bud carefully picked up the long, sheathed object and secured it in the top of his rucksack. He lifted the bag onto his back but warned the others not to get too close as the object was dangerously poking out from either side of the top flap.

'You'd better be worth it,' he announced to the "treasure."

They took a few deep breaths to control their breathing and painstakingly moved back down the original tunnel trying not to trip over the rails in the dark and always squinting ahead towards the faint beam of light – occasionally glancing backwards into the darkness.

They called out loud for Mickey every so often, worried sick as to what had happened to him. Kall moved as quickly as he dared through the tunnel, with Blip trying to follow him and Bud bringing up the rear in order to avoid poking anyone with the treasured object. Eventually, Kall approached the faint light and as he had hoped, found the other torch lying on the ground next to the stone steps which led upwards to the tower. By now, the batteries had almost drained and there was only a slight glow, which didn't help much in their search for Mickey so Blip changed the batteries again. Kall and Bud moved carefully over to the rail trucks to see if he was hiding anywhere near them. They searched around, shining the torch into any dark corners, while quietly but urgently, calling his name.

Blip resting shakily on the bottom step, heard a slight mumbling behind him which caused him some alarm until he realised it was Mickey making unintelligible noises. He stretched out his hands in the darkness to try to work out exactly where Mickey was and called over to the others. 'He's here – I think he's fallen – he doesn't sound very good.'

The other two went over quickly and found Mickey lying crumpled on the lower steps where he had obviously slipped in his panic. The light of the torch showed up a big cut on his forehead with blood dripping into his eyes. He was slowly starting to regain consciousness and was becoming more and more agitated as he realised he had become momentarily blinded by both the darkness and his eyes being gummed up.

'Here's the infamous hanky again,' muttered Bud and pulled Blip's hanky from his own pocket where he had quickly stuffed it. 'Useful for something I suppose!' Bud tried to wipe the blood away from Mickey's eyes as he slowly regained consciousness.

'Oh thanks Bud, I don't think I want it back any more,' Blip grimaced at the sight of his hanky now smeared with Mickey's blood (among other things).

Mickey started to grasp Bud's arm in agitation 'Don't let it come close – not again – please keep it away!'

'Come on lads, if Mickey can manage, we need to get out of here... now!' Kall kept looking over his shoulder into the darkness.

'But something chased it away, didn't it? We all heard the wings beating again. Whatever it was – it chased it away!' Blip's blood pressure was rising again and he tried to breathe slowly to stop the rising panic.

'That doesn't mean it won't return and try again,' Kall announced. 'We have walked off with whatever it was guarding ... haven't we?' he added as he looked curiously at the mysterious shape at the top of Bud's rucksack.

'Ok let's go. Blip – take the torch and then you lead the way. Kall can you help Mickey? I'll come last otherwise I'm going to poke somebody's eye out with this thing.' Bud indicated the 'treasure'.

They were now all looking over their shoulders and listening carefully to the ominous echoes which had once more started to drift around the tunnels. Blip fumbled for the torch from Kall's hand and immediately started up the steep stone steps. Kall followed – almost dragging Mickey to his feet and half carrying him as he scraped his elbows every time he had to balance against the slabbed wall. Bud tried to manoeuvre himself up the narrow steps, twisting sideways in order to stop scraping his bulky rucksack against the wall. On one occasion, when he almost fell, he thought he caught the sound of metal scraping against stone and wondered curiously just what he was carrying.

It was a long way. For some unaccountable reason there seemed to be more steps going up than when they descended which caused Blip to groan every time he turned a bend and realised there were still more steps. 'Not there yet' he panted.

Bud was getting more nervous and felt that he was being followed. 'Hurry up Blip. Are you ok Kall? Is it getting a bit lighter?' His breath seemed to come in spasms and not just through the exertion of the climb. His skin was crawling in fear and trepidation.

'We're there!' Blip called back down the shaft as he crawled through the still open entrance. He helped to pull Mickey through the narrow gap and then lay panting while Kall emerged rather more quickly than he intended, propelled by Bud who as the last in line, was still essentially in the dark and wanting to get out into the open. He still couldn't get rid of the feeling that something was creeping up the steps.

CHAPTER SIXTEEN

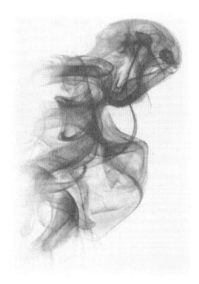

K all rubbed his scraped elbows as they all blinked in the sudden bright light of the sun, shining through one of the circular window apertures in the tower. However, there was still a cold draught and a musty aroma emanating from the shaft. Kall quickly tried to find a way to cover or close the ominous dark entrance to the stairwell which was still gaping open like a hungry mouth. He glanced down the steps and gasped in fear as a small spiral of black smoke appeared around the nearest bend in the stairwell ... and surely there were there two coal black eyes staring fixedly at him? He lurched back so suddenly that he and Bud landed on the floor in a heap.

'Quick ... Quick!' He yelped in panic and begged for some help. He tried to tug the stone hatchway into position with Bud's help and they all eventually heard the small, hidden lever click shut.

Mickey sobbed quietly in relief and Blip looked away, a little embarrassed, as a lonely tear trickled down his own dirty cheek. They all got up as soon as they could get their breath back. and helping Mickey, who was still shaky and stumbling over his own feet, they made their way down as quickly as they could, to where their ponies were hobbled and were patiently eating any grass within reach. Kall prepared the ponies for a quick getaway while the others collected their belongings and Bud wiped Mickey's forehead again after rinsing the inevitable filthy hanky with some clean water.

A soft incessant drumming attracted their attention and they all turned to face Kall who had sat down on a convenient boulder and was tapping out a repetitive ostinato on his drum. The sound grew louder and more intense and seemed to throb and reverberate around the entire surrounding area. He paused and then repeated the rhythms. The coda changed tempo and became more nervous and agitated. The boys looked questioningly at him.

'Just telling the village that the quest is solved and we are safe ... for now,' he added.

'Wow – will the sound carry that far?' Blip asked.

'You'd be surprised. It is one of the best ways to send messages on the island.'

'So much for your phone, Blip,' Bud attempted to tease, but he wasn't really in the mood.

Kall started to sling the drum over Sage's back while the others' prepared to mount the other reliable and sturdy ponies. A slight change in the light – a cloud over the sun made them look up at the tower in trepidation. At the top of the ruined turret, a hint of black smoke seeped and curled, growing in strength and intensity. It arose high out of the tower as their mouths fell open in dismay. The smoke curled and wavered – formless, yet evil. The ground around the tower shook and a black, hissing demonic form started to take shape until a malevolent, wraith–like figure gradually emerged and came into focus, writhing out of the smoke which was by now towering high above the ruined turret.

Kall started to mutter under his breath in panic, 'the vagous wraith, the Nyxx – the plague.'

Bud started to mutter too, but his words were spoken inwardly ... a plea for help ... a plea for deliverance. Blip and Mickey were white with horror and fright. They shielded their eyes and leant against Guru seeking comfort wherever it could be found. The Nyxx gradually moved from a formless void to the personification of all their worst nightmares. Indistinct facial features, both evil and proud, started to become clearer and two lifeless, coal-black eyes slowly rotated to gaze at the boys.

'Don't look – don't look – turn away!' screamed Kall and he too hid his eyes in Sage's mane. Blip and Mickey sobbed in fright and pulled Guru even closer to them. The sturdy pony seemed to be a barrier between themselves and the Nyxx.

Bud started to suspect that the demonic creature was searching for him. He had been the one who had carried the treasure away. He still had his rucksack on his back with the burden of it weighing him down more and more. It seemed to drag him downwards. Those eyes slowly turned to seek him out and he started to shake uncontrollably.

He was still muttering under his breath, but Bud was unable to control his physical actions against this evil power and he fell, helpless to his feet. He tried to blot out all sight of those empty black eyes searching for him alone. Icy fingers seemed to stroke his mind – persuading, beguiling, coaxing him to look up, to meet those eyes. He started to raise his head, but stopped when he heard what he thought was the sound of hoof beats approaching in the distance.

The Nyxx hesitated for just one second and then renewed her harsh anger when she realised it was Kall, steadily drumming once more, only this time it was a more insistent rhythm – a galloping rhythm – a rhythm that built to a crescendo and was meant to signify the arrival of salvation and deliverance. The Nyxx was steadily forcing Bud's mind to turn his head and meet her inky black eyes. But by now he realised with a desperate hope, that the sound of the drumming hoof beats was essentially a request for help. Bud hoped it would arrive in time as he felt his mind being possessed, controlled and captured.

The same blinding, searing flash of light they had witnessed in the mine, made him shout out in agony just as the creature screamed and shrieked again like a tortured banshee. The earth grew silent apart from that one unearthly, agonising screech which echoed around for miles. The smoke whirled away, spitting like a vicious, black firecracker and then disappeared from sight. The boys covered their ears in agony and pain and blinked vigorously to clear their eyesight after the blazing flash.

Scout couldn't cope with all the unexpected sights and sounds any longer and he bucked and leapt forwards into a frenzied gallop, whinnying and screeching in wide-eyed panic. He ran straight for the cliff and disappeared from sight with a final primeval scream of fear. Silence reigned as the boys froze ... hardly daring to speak or move.

Slowly, gradually, the birds started to tweet hesitantly at first and then with more confidence. The boys slowly uncurled themselves from their positions of relative safety and glanced at each other in horror. Kall sobbed, 'Oh no ... oh no ... Scout! Sula will never forgive me. Oh Scout!' He scuttled towards the cliff with Bud and Blip following – Mickey was sitting on the ground staring at his hands now smeared with the blood from his still bleeding forehead.

The boys approached the cliff and nervously gazed over the edge expecting to see the battered body of the pony on the rocks below. Scout had slipped a long way but had come to rest rather miraculously on a narrow scree path. Yet even as they watched and tried to work out how to rescue the young pony, he started to slip further down the slope – his eyes wide in fear. The halter had become entangled in a large clump of bracken and for the moment helped to hold him on the path ... but they could see it wouldn't last long.

'I'll go down,' Kall decided. 'He knows me.'

'But he'll pull you over with him if he panics,' Bud warned.

'Well what can I do? I can't just abandon Sula's pony – I have to try.' Kall looked determined. He moved to the edge and started to talk gently to Scout trying to reassure the nervous pony. When he thought the pony had got used to his presence he gradually descended the cliff, being careful to keep to one side in case he dislodged any stones. Scout whickered and tried to pull away at one point – but Kall's voice managed to reassure the pony once more. After what seemed to be an eternity, he managed to arrive alongside and slowly and deftly untangled the halter from the bracken, but putting himself in more danger in the process. There was now nothing to support them on the cliff face and the scree was starting to move and slither away.

Scout refused to move. Whatever coaxing and reassurance Kall gave, to try to get the pony to move slowly up the narrow path ... Scout completely ignored him. The pony started to move his hooves to gain a more secure position, which sent another load of stones tumbling down the cliff and Scout started plunging in fright with Kall hanging onto the halter.

Bud and Blip suddenly looked around as they thought they heard Kall's drum beating its' incessant ostinato – but this time it really was the approach of hooves galloping towards them. They clutched each other wondering what new danger was approaching them now. Bud glanced over to his rucksack wondering how quickly he could get to it, when a horse and rider appeared at the edge of the forest. Bud and Blip both gazed open-mouthed as they recognised the startling figure of Uriel, golden-streaked hair flowing out behind him, seated bareback on the most beautiful, pale dappled horse.

Uriel cantered Aisling up towards them while they both gobbled like turkeycocks.

'Wha ... when... how did...?' Blip couldn't manage a full sentence in his shock.

Bud however, felt his suspicions were now confirmed and permitted himself a small smile of satisfaction. He nodded a brief welcome to the pale rider. Uriel smiled – lighting his whole face, even more dazzling than the sun shining high in the sky.

He propelled Aisling towards the cliff edge and quickly slid off the horse's back. Aisling carefully planted sure-footed hooves in the heather and whickered to the frightened pony below.

Kall was stunned and stood frozen into immobility, thinking that all the local legends he had been taught in his childhood had now come to life and stood proudly on the cliff edge above him. He gazed in shock until Uriel met his eyes and smiled encouragingly at the youth. 'Come ... it is time for all of you to return home. You have done well.'

Aisling whinnied once more.

Scout and Kall felt the undeniable magnetism emanating from both Aisling and Uriel and they carefully began to make their way along the steep path. The eyes of the pony and youth never left their ultimate goal. When they finally achieved safety, Kall's eyes were shining like bright stars and Scout immediately approached the regal dappled horse, whickering softly in greeting.

Uriel approached Kall. He gripped his shoulder reassuringly and Kall felt all his fears ebb away in the presence of this pale, yet almost iridescent young man. 'You have done well,' Uriel repeated. He then approached Bud and smiled... 'You remembered ... *"I'll be there when you entreat me and all darkness overthrow."'*

'I wasn't sure there for a second .... Tell me ... are you ...?' Bud began.

'Now is not the time Bud ... *She* and her servants are still close by. Remember – *"She'll pursue your heart - until you're free."'*

Blip had found the use of his vocal chords by now and grimaced ... 'Oh no, Uriel, don't start spouting poetry again.'

Uriel smiled, 'Ok Blip – but have faith and remember ..."*The chest holds more than just one key."'*

'Uh – what's that supposed to mean?'

'Just remember, Blip ... Nice new trouser design by the way... plenty of ventilation!'

Uriel turned to look for Mickey and walked slowly over to the frightened boy sitting on the ground near the other ponies. He knelt beside him as Mickey nervously lifted his head to see who or what was approaching him now. Uriel spoke quietly and earnestly for a while as he inspected Mickey's forehead with one gentle hand. Mickey was seen to nod in agreement and presently, Uriel stood up to call the other boys over.

The three of them quickly approached Uriel, with Kall leading Scout. Aisling was trotting alongside, whickering reassuringly at Scout every time the pony twisted his head around so he could see whether his dappled friend was following. Uriel helped a rather bemused and shy Mickey to his feet and although Mickey wouldn't meet the eyes of the other boys – he kept glancing with a mixture of respect and curiosity at Uriel.

The boys collected their meagre belongings and quickly mounted the ponies. Blip tugged Mickey up behind him rather more gently than before and didn't even make a comment when Mickey clutched at the waistband of his jeans. Uriel, almost reverently, picked up Bud's backpack with the wrapped object still protruding from either side of the top flap. Meanwhile, Bud mounted Scout – now calmly eating a mouthful of grass.

'Don't you want the item now ... the treasure?' Bud asked carefully as Uriel helped Bud to shoulder the bulkily-shaped rucksack.

'The quest was given to you,' Uriel included all the boys in his gesture. 'It must be fulfilled.' Uriel leapt lightly onto Aisling's back and faced the boys. 'There is still danger and you must all return to your families as soon as possible. I want you to go straight to the beach and to the chest. If you can, wait there in safety – I will send Batty and Wayne to you as quickly as I can.'

'There is only one beach in that direction, near the mouth of the river,' indicated Kall. 'I will lead them along the coast – I know the path well.'

'Very well, but you all need to take care as danger is still near at hand. Do not get distracted by anyone or anything ... speed is now important.' Uriel was firm but nodded towards Kall in agreement. He turned Aisling and with one bound they galloped into the forest, following the narrow path back to Mowl. 'Be swift,' echoed through the trees and a sudden blinding flash spurred the boys into action.

'We must go quickly,' called Kall. 'I will have to lead, but let's put Scout next – he has already had one fright today. Guru will follow safely,' he reassured Mickey and Blip.

Mickey wasn't happy about being at the back, but for once Blip was sympathetic. 'Hang onto me Mickey ... I'm here.'

They all nudged their ponies into a far quicker pace than before and held tightly to their shaggy manes, as the path twisted and turned awkwardly, following the cliff edge. Bud, now holding on for dear life, was worried about the *treasure* bouncing around in his backpack – but kept his worries to himself as he noticed that Kall was carrying his loaded crossbow in one hand while he guided Sage with his knees, and the other hand held on tightly to the halter. Bud wished he had had the forethought to find his dagger before they had set off and he started to stare around him as they moved swiftly down the path. He gazed at the nearby treeline and occasionally glanced behind him to check that Blip and Mickey were still ok.

The autumn sun warmed their backs as they swiftly made their way along the track. The ponies picked their way down the meandering coastal path as it descended from the steep cliffs down to the sand dunes. The view towards the sea was breathtakingly beautiful, but the boys had no time to look. Mickey was hanging on for dear life and Blip's eyes were staring fixedly at Bud's back and Scout's flaxen tail, so that he was prepared for any sudden sideways movement from Guru. They were following so closely behind the others, Guru's nose was almost touching Scout's rump.

Bud was nervous. The ominously dark treeline was close on their left and occasionally they trotted through the edge of the forest and wound their way through a few sporadic trees. The silently menacing forest felt malignant and forbidding, but the path wouldn't allow for any more than a quick trot at this point.

In an instant – everything changed. Bud had glanced sideways for a second as he caught the glimpse of something moving in the trees. Unfortunately it was at the same time that Kall took them in between two rather gnarled trunks almost blocking their path.

'Watch out Bud!' Blip's cry of warning came too late for Bud and one long leg caught on a low branch – twisting him around slightly and the long object still protruding from either side of his rucksack smacked squarely into the two trees and brought his forward motion to an abrupt halt. Scout managed to squeeze his rather rotund belly between the trees and Bud somersaulted inelegantly backwards, straight over Scout's rather beautiful tail. Guru lurched sideways in surprise as a lanky body flew towards his nose, and Blip and Mickey went in entirely the opposite direction and slid clumsily and unexpectedly into the base of one of the trees. They ended up still poised in their riding positions with Mickey holding tightly onto Blip's belt.

'Argh! Gerroff ... now!' Blip scrambled away from Mickey's vice-like grip.

'Hey are you all ok?' Kall had stopped a little further down the track and was looking backwards in concern. 'Bud? You ok?'

Kall was intrigued by Bud's rather suspicious movements as he dropped behind the two trees without warning and shushed the other boys. Bud signalled the others to join him in hiding, but Kall was still on mounted on Sage and was in the middle of the track. Kall tentatively looked around, following the direction of Bud's pointing finger. He held his breath and laid a warning hand on Sage's neck while the other hand tightly gripped his cross-bow. He gazed into the forest as Bud had indicated.

'What is it Bud?' asked Blip worriedly.

'Ooh – oh n-no,' Mickey was heard to mutter to himself in trepidation.

'Shush, I saw something moving.' Bud slowly slid his hand into his backpack and drew out the dagger, feeling more confident with it resting in his grip. Blip took one look at him and did the same. Mickey tried to grab the dagger and a short struggle ensued until Bud hissed angrily at Mickey. 'Stop it! Keep still!'

They all froze with fright as a dirty, unkempt man emerged slowly out of the forest and shuffled in the direction of the boys, an ugly smirk transforming his face into an evil grimace and greasy hair hanging over his sightless, opaque left eye. His right eye, with a hideous scar puckering his upper eyelid tried to focus on Kall holding Sage in readiness, and then slowly and menacingly moved on, searching the undergrowth for his intended victim ... Bud.

He paused and ominously sniffed the air in all directions taking small steps forward and again trying to 'scent' his prey. Merrick had been sent to destroy the *thief.*

CHAPTER SEVENTEEN

Batty had tried to keep herself as busy as possible, so that she didn't have much time to think about the situations Bud and Blip might experience. She was starting to get increasingly worried about how long it was taking and whether her parents had already discovered that they were all missing.

'It'll be alright Batty,' Wayne tried to reassure her. 'They'll be back soon.'

Wayne had made great progress after Uriel's visit and was almost back to normal. His eyes seemed brighter and his manner less stressed. He and Batty had also become firm friends and spent a lot of time walking Bluebell and sauntering together by the river, chatting about whatever came into their minds... elder brothers, school, dogs. They laughingly discussed cricket at one point.

Sula was often with them but stayed close to Jalen at other times, discussing the unexpected appearance of Uriel and some of the frightening and confusing things that had happened. Sula was missing Kall and also the presence of her pony, Scout.

That night, the same night the boys were sleeping outside the Linnaeus tower, Jalen kept guard by sleeping in the doorway of the hut which meant that Sula, Batty and Wayne managed to catch up on some sleep and passed a relatively calm night. Bluebell slept cuddled up between Sula and Batty.

The next morning they let Jalen sleep while the three of them prepared some food for their meals and helped a few villagers to keep the fire burning by collecting some more wood. They didn't stray far from the village however, and still eyed the depths of the forest with suspicion and dread. Batty spent a lot of the time either on the lookout for the boys, or keeping a close eye on Bluebell. She wasn't happy when she saw Merrick shuffle into Mowl village and start to slobber and devour some leftover food. He sat down by the fire and smirked spitefully when he saw Batty holding tightly onto Bluebell's collar.

The day passed slowly as they waited impatiently for the boys to return. They kept watch near to the track which led out of the village towards the tower, and listened for any sign or sound that would herald the return of the ponies. The sun rose higher in the clear autumn sky and Batty started to feel even more nervous as the time seemed to pass so slowly.

'Kall knows the way really well, Batty, they'll be all right.' Sula tried to reassure her new friend and convince herself at the same time.

'I know, but they don't know what they are going to find and they don't know how dangerous it will be,' Batty complained.

'It will be dangerous – just think what tried to approach us yesterday!' Wayne was not feeling too diplomatic. The darkness still brought on his dread of the malevolent plague which had swept over him, when he had been lost in the forest with his brother.

'Thanks for that reassurance, Wayne,' Batty said sarcastically. Bluebell tried to reassure her young mistress by licking the only place that was on her own height, which happened to be the back of Batty's knees. 'Thanks Bluey!'

'No, I didn't mean it that way Batty ... what I meant was ...' Wayne took a deep breath, 'it will be dangerous ... but Uriel will be around to guard them.' He smiled a little shyly at Batty.

'He might not have been going that way; he might have other things to do.' Batty whined a little plaintively. Bluebell whined back which made Batty smile.

'But they only have to ask,' remarked Wayne faithfully and he quoted ...
'"I'll be there when you entreat me and all darkness overthrow."'

Batty thought for a few seconds and then smiled back. 'Thanks Wayne, you are right ... we must remember they only have to ask. It is like Uriel is looking out for us.'

Twice in the next few hours – Jalen emerged quickly from the hut and rushed to the edge of the clearing and stood listening carefully. In the distance, the thrumming of a small drum could be heard, interrupting the high-pitched twittering of birdsong and the bleat of hungry lambs. Jalen stood stock still for a few seconds as he interpreted the rhythms and then returned to the hut to report that the boys were safe and had completed the quest. Sula and Batty sighed in relief, but Wayne nudged Batty to attract her attention as he observed Merrick disappearing down the path which led in the direction of the tower. He may have been limping, yet he still moved with some urgency ... as if he had been called.

However the second time he heard the drums, Jalen returned downcast and with bowed head. 'Kall is drumming the rhythm that asks for aid. They must be in some trouble.'

'Can't we help?' asked Batty in concern.

'We won't get there for some time, but we must try to see what is wrong.' He called a few villagers together and after some rapid preparations, they set off down the same rough track Merrick had chosen earlier. Batty grabbed Bluebell again as she strained to follow the men.

Time passed even more slowly and Batty lay back in the dusty clearing and squinted at the sun moving slowly towards the west. She tried counting the white fluffy clouds to pass the time.

'Shh! What's that?' Sula held a hand up for silence. They all listened carefully – straining their ears to catch any sounds.

In the distance the thud of hooves could be heard – but this wasn't a drum message, and as the hoof beats approached the clearing it was obvious it wasn't a pony, it was a horse cantering quickly towards the village. The three of them stood up and gazed expectantly down the first part of the track, to where it disappeared into the deeper and darker part of the forest. They gripped each other's hands without realising and held their breath in anticipation.

The sound of the hoof beats grew louder and closer until around the corner, white mane and tail flowing, Aisling appeared with Uriel bending down low over the horse's neck to avoid the low branches clutching at his arms and head. Uriel's hair looked windswept and ruffled as Aisling drew level with the three startled children, skidded to a halt and Uriel flung himself lightly from the sweating horse.

Some of the remaining villagers came out to look but kept their distance from the visitor, almost as if they were too shy to come forward. With Bluebell in the lead, Wayne, Batty and Sula welcomed Uriel with pleasure – although they were also a little in awe of the vibrant, shining youth. Bluebell just went charging up to him and leapt up at him so that he had to catch her paw in his hands to fend her off. She whined at him as if to tell him again ... all about her earlier misadventure.

'Uriel – are they all ok?' Batty asked quickly. 'Do you know if they are safe?' She looked closely at Uriel as he smiled at her in order to reassure her.

'They are safe for now. They have fulfilled the quest, they have the treasure ... and they must now keep it safe and return home.' Uriel paused and Batty quickly picked up on his hesitation.

'They are safe for now? Does that mean they could still be in some kind of danger?' Batty asked nervously.

'*She'll pursue your heart - until you're free,*' Uriel quoted. 'We must get you, Wayne and Bluebell to the beach as quickly as possible so that you can all ... be free.'

'It's a long way to the beach, Uriel,' said Sula shyly.

'I know Sula ... Batty, Wayne! Collect your belongings together now please.' He added ominously, 'Aisling will carry you faster than anything else. Nothing will be able to catch you.'

Batty looked at him closely but went to collect her bag and jacket from the hut without speaking. Sula however had other thoughts.

'They must eat something before they go, Uriel.'

'Then they need to do so quickly,' came the response.

Sula rushed to prepare some basic food rations while Wayne sat near the village fire and talked shyly with Uriel. Bluebell kept trying to climb on Uriel's knee for reassurance.

Batty helped Sula to carry the food to the camp fire and they all sat down to refresh themselves with meat, eggs, bread and some forest fruits. Batty and Wayne then went to fill a crude container with some fresh water while Bluebell had a long drink from the river. Sula had the envious task of rubbing Aisling down and feeding her some fresh oatmeal.

When Wayne and Batty returned from the river Sula was wearing the widest grin they had ever seen while Aisling whickered gently and nuzzled her hands, wanting more attention. She stroked the horse's elegant nose and soft muzzle while singing gently to her. Aisling had her ears pricked and was listening intently to the soft sounds until Uriel rose effortlessly to his feet. He moved to Sula's side to check that Aisling had recovered enough to travel swiftly to the beach.

'Come, you must go now. You must not delay any longer.'

'Aren't you coming with us?' Wayne asked warily.

'Aisling can carry the two of you and Bluebell, swiftly. You are not heavy – with me on her back she will not be so swift.' Uriel smiled in order to reassure them. 'Aisling will keep you safe, you will not fall.' Uriel helped them to mount – Batty in front and Wayne holding on tightly behind her while Sula stood at the horse's head, not wanting to let go.

Bluebell was lifted up in front of Batty, wrapped tightly in her jacket. She was secured with a leather strap fastened around Batty's back in order to help keep her secure. Bluebell struggled to get her legs free. 'No Bluey you have to keep still. Keep still girl – I've got you.'

Uriel approached Bluebell and spoke very quietly and simply to her … telling her to remain calm. He held his finger out and touched her nose in order to maintain her focus. Bluebell immediately licked Uriel's finger as if to say, 'It is ok – I'll be good!' He chuckled, then smiled and stroked her forehead. Uriel then showed Batty how to grip the strong but silky mane, twisting it around her hand.

'Uriel…?' Batty started to speak, 'Will you … Are you …?'

'Not now Batty – now is not the time.'

'You've said that before,' Batty was getting a little impatient and indignant.

'I also meant it before.' Uriel held her hand firmly and she immediately grew calm and still under his impelling touch. 'Now is not the time … the next stage of your journey is too urgent. We will talk when the quest is entire and whole ... and, I venture to say – perfect.' Uriel released her hand and she almost felt bereft, as if something was missing in her life.

'Sula ...' Batty called to her friend. The lump in her throat was too big to allow her to thank her new friend so she leant over Aisling's back and grasped her hand tightly. She looked deeply into the other girl's heart.

'I know Batty. Please come back to see us – I will miss you ... so much ... so much,' Sula whispered, a tear slowly rolled down her cheek.

'Sula... I will never, ever forget how much you have helped me. You saved my life. I can never repay you. I hope we will meet again.' Wayne gulped and sobbed quietly ... looking away in embarrassment.

Uriel took control. 'Don't look to the side. Keep looking for the path – Aisling will keep you safe.' He gave last minute instructions to the two of them and then spoke a few quiet words to the beautiful, dappled horse. He pointed Aisling towards the track that led eventually to the beach and lightly patted the horse's rump. Aisling immediately stepped forward and began what they all hoped was their final journey.

Left behind in the village clearing, Uriel watched their progress carefully until they crossed the river near the stepping stones and trotted out of sight. He turned to say a quick farewell to Sula and to Jalen, who had just returned to the village without finding the boys. He then swiftly disappeared into the forest via a rarely used pathway. Sula and Jalen were left staring after him in bewilderment.

* * *

Aisling trotted at first until they had forded the river and then broke into a slow careful, canter until Batty and Wayne started to settle into the rhythm of her stride. Then as the sun flickered between the branches and the gloom of the forest started to envelop them, Aisling lengthened her stride. Batty talked endlessly to Bluebell to let her know she was still with her, while she stared ahead and concentrated on the path while the trees sped past. Wayne was holding on for dear life and had his face tucked into Batty's backpack so he couldn't have looked sideways even if he had wanted to do so.

The journey passed swiftly but it soon became noticeable that the clouds and the darkness were crowding out the sunlight far too early. At the start of one very long section of path stretching ahead of them like roman road, Batty suddenly felt Aisling slow right down and prick her ears up. She shivered uncontrollably and Wayne picked his head up.

'What's happening?' he whispered. The forest had gone quiet and there was none of the usual birdsong punctuating the rustling of the leaves.

'Quiet … something's wrong.' Batty squinted ahead but could see nothing. Bluebell hid her face and whimpered. 'It's ok Bluebell,' she whispered.

The sea breeze had also dropped and the air was still, but it was not calm as in a peaceful autumn evening – it was dark and murky and menacing. Aisling whickered very softly but continued to walk along the path. Batty thought she imagined a wisp of dark smoke passing between the trees in the distance. Aisling stopped for a second – her nostrils quivering as she scented the air ahead.

Nothing moved. The forest seemed devoid of all life and Batty and Wayne hardly dared to breathe. The horse suddenly moved forward nearly unseating them and the riders both tightened their grip on each other. Aisling gathered her legs beneath her and set off like an arrow along the narrow track.

They didn't stop for anything. The forest grew darker and darker until they could hardly see ahead of them, yet the pale horse seemed to almost glow in the dark. The track widened out and the trees grew further apart and still the horse galloped on. The smell of salt on the air and the sound of waves pounding the beach could just be sensed in the gloomy atmosphere when suddenly there were flashing lights and shrieks and screams, echoing in the darkness.

A foul smell on the air made them gag with disgust and Wayne clutched at Batty. Aisling didn't hesitate but slowed to a steady and deliberate canter, looking from side to side and gathering herself – ready to change direction at a moment's notice. Batty moaned in distress as to what they would find when they reached their destination.

More dazzling lights and yells punctuated the darkness until a stunning beam of light pierced the gloomy sky, like a magnificent searchlight. Aisling skidded to a halt and within seconds a terrifying, black whirlwind of oppressive smoke almost swept the riders from Aisling's unyielding back. Wayne leant forward to grasp Batty's free hand and she, in turn, bent protectively over Bluebell's shivering body. A loathsome, inhuman shape followed the smoke and approached them at breakneck speed, its mouth gaping open and coal black eyes almost incandescent with shock. A shrill howl set up startling vibrations through Aisling's back as the phantom plunged straight through their bodies making them gasp for air.

'Don't look at her eyes Batty – Don't look!' Wayne almost screamed. But the 'Nyxx' had fled into the gloomy forest, still shrieking loudly.

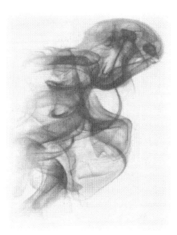

Slowly, perceptively – the fearful echoes died away and the oppressive atmosphere began to lift. The sun peeped through the clouds and the black mood that had overtaken them was lazily swept away, dissolving into insignificance with the warmth and glow.

Batty gave a huge sigh of relief and Wayne started to giggle which made Batty chuckle too ... until they all heard a faint, but obviously very nervous whinny, up ahead. Batty immediately stopped and turned her head to look nervously at Wayne.

'Oh Wayne – what can have happened?' she wailed. 'I h–hope they are all safe.'

'Let's go and see ... they'll be ok .... I hope ... but they might need help,' he added.

She met his troubled eyes just as Aisling started moving again – this time lifting her hooves in a steady trot. After a couple of minutes, she took the corner leading onto the beach as if they were just out for a daily ride, although a closer inspection would notice her sides were heaving with the recent effort.

Bluebell's black nose timidly poked out of Batty's jacket, twitching slightly as she sniffed the air. Batty and Wayne glanced tentatively across the beach, afraid of what they would discover.

CHAPTER EIGHTEEN

Merrick had been sent to destroy the *thief*.

Kall remained still and watchful, not wanting to give away Bud's whereabouts – but ready to intervene if necessary. Sage stood like a statue as Kall surreptitiously brought the loaded crossbow up ready to aim. Guru and Scout had ended up grazing quietly near the pathway while waiting for their errant riders to appear and remount.

Merrick sneered spitefully at Kall – then ignored him and shuffled forwards, 'scenting' the air and aiming straight for the hidden boys. Kall's attention was distracted for a second as he saw a slight movement out of the corner of his eye. He stared fixedly at the edge of the dismal, shadowy forest and noticed a small wisp of black smoke start to swirl around some protruding branches. The smoky tendrils seemed to almost clasp the tree for support as they gradually forged together and started to establish the more menacing and threatening female manifestation. The shape kept shifting in the shadowy gloom but never moved forward into the bright sunlight.

'The Nyxx,' Kall whispered to himself and then waiting no longer, he sparked into sudden violent activity. 'Bud! Blip! Mickey! Now – we have to go now! Mount up quickly and stay in the sunlight.'

Sage responded immediately to Kall's heels and plunged towards the boys and the approaching 'wall-eyed' drudge, still scenting the air around him. Kall didn't hesitate but let one of his crudely sharpened arrows fly at Merrick – the cross-bow's taut spring sending the bolt straight at the man's legs. Merrick went down with a shriek of agony as the stubby arrow hit him in the left knee, partly severing a tendon in his lower leg. A shriek of anger and frustration could be heard from the edge of the forest.

'Scout, Guru!' Kall called the ponies to him as he kneed Sage into a protective position between the boys and the forest. He leant low over Sage's shoulder and grabbed the dangling halters of the two startled ponies. The boys, equally startled, had not wasted any time and had leapt to their feet grabbing the pony's rugs and their own belongings. Kall rushed the ponies over to the boys who were all agitatedly scrambling towards him over some precariously placed boulders.

Bud was very careful when swinging his rucksack back on his shoulders and after stepping onto Scout's back from a boulder – he made sure he guided Scout around the trees which he imagined had deliberately felled him. Blip leapt neatly onto Guru's back but Mickey in his panic was not so agile and was left snatching and grasping Guru's tail as Blip tried to canter off after the others. Guru came to sudden halt and whinnied indignantly at the sudden agonising tug.

'Blip – wait for me – wait – don't leave me!' Mickey whimpered and cried out in his panic. He looked over his shoulder as he heard grunts and groans coming from the undergrowth and screamed as Merrick's face slowly appeared over the top of a tree stump, his mouth distorted into a slobbering grimace and his damaged, but still malevolent eye searching and seeking for his prey. A second angry shriek could be heard from the smoky apparition, almost camouflaged by the tree line.

'Come on Mickey for God's sake – stop lolling around on the grass – and stop holding Guru's tail or he'll kick you!' Blip kept searching the skyline for any sign of approaching menace and then kept glancing at Merrick still struggling to reach them. 'Ugh!' he said in revulsion at the sight of the dirty, greasy man. He reached an arm down and hauled Mickey onto Guru's back behind him, calling out in pain as Mickey's vice-like grip grasped him around the waist. 'Ow! Stop it Mickey I can't breathe properly!'

But Mickey was still panting and making small uncontrollable whimpers in his fear and panic. 'Don't leave me – I'm coming with you – You have to take me with you!' Bud and Kall had both galloped off and were some distance away, but Bud reined in Scout and called back to reassure them both.

'Come on quickly, it's all ok, Merrick can't follow us now ... but we need to get out of here. Guru will catch us up. Just keep hanging on. Hold onto his mane Blip!' Bud kept looking anxiously towards the forest but there was no sign of them being followed in the bright afternoon sunshine. Blip held tightly onto the mane and kneed Guru with his heels. The pony lunged forwards while Mickey grunted and clasped Blip even more tightly.

Kall led the way and the other ponies followed in their own sure-footed way down the winding, rugged pathways. Speed was important and Kall kept them moving at a fast canter which rattled their teeth and shook their bones like a couple of skeletons mounted on a Valkyrie's horse ... as Blip later complained.

After an hour of tense riding, they eventually approached one side of the river – named by Kall as the river Thell, and let the ponies rest briefly while they all drink some of the clear bubbling water and refilled their bottles. Mickey was so rattled and stressed he threw up in a nearby bush.

'Oh gross!' Blip wasn't feeling very sympathetic. 'But I'm glad you waited until we stopped and didn't do that down the back of my neck!' he said consolingly.

'Sorry Blip. Sorry Bud, Kall.' Mickey was feeling really forlorn, but perhaps with good reason. In the space of a few days and nights he had been stranded in a forest where his brother had caught a deadly plague, been petrified and spooked by perilous manifestations he didn't understand and had received a really nasty bump on the head. Yet he hadn't forgotten what to him, was still the most important part of the quest. 'Shall we have a look at the *treasure* now then?'

'No we won't,' said Blip.

'We need to get it home first Mickey,' stated Bud.

'How are we going to get home anyway?' Mickey sneered sarcastically.

'You'll see.' Bud wasn't very forthcoming.

'We are not safe yet Mickey, Uriel said we need to get back to the beach.' Kall was still gazing around him, still on the alert for any unexpected threat.

'So who is the guy – and why isn't he here protecting us?'

Bud ignored the first part of the question and stated firmly, 'he is fetching Wayne and Batty and Bluebell.' He added … 'We just need to keep safe until they manage to join us at the beach.'

After refreshing themselves, they remounted, then paddled the ponies across a shallow part of the river and cantered down a wider path towards the coast, hoping to see the relative safety of the beach. Bud and Blip quickly urged their ponies past the crude shelter they had erected on that first terrifying night, nervously looking all around them. But they soon left the darkest part of the forest far behind and found the ground becoming increasingly soft and sandy. The trees became sparser and larger patches of blue sky appeared up ahead. The breeze grew stronger and carried the salt smell of the sea towards them. Their spirits lifted.

Blip could hardly believe it when they trotted down a narrow section of stony path which opened out onto the beach, so soon after leaving the forest. Surely it had taken a long time to walk the same distance? They all carefully dismounted, stretched their aching and sore legs and led the ponies towards the sand dunes a short distance away from a set of tall conifers lining the beach. Blip's bare leg was a bit red where he had struggled to stay on Guru's sturdy back and his delicate skin was chafed. He winced as he started to rub the inside of his knee – but then his attention was drawn elsewhere and he started to grin and chuckle when he realised that his *signpost* was still in place, marking the spot where they had left the chest. He was about to wipe off the sand and seaweed, and pull the clods of grass off the top of the hidden chest when Bud held a hand up in warning.

'No Blip, let's leave it hidden for a while until Batty and Wayne arrive anyway.'

'Leave what hidden? You're not hiding more treasure are you?' Mickey moved towards the hidden chest and spitefully kicked away the large pebbles and stick with his foot. He bent down to investigate the curious mound of sand, seaweed and grass and found himself thrown roughly to the ground by a furious red whirlwind, spitting with anger and impatience.

'I've had enough! Stop poking your nose in where it is not wanted! Leave our things alone – or we WILL leave you here!' Blip had leapt on top of Mickey and was punctuating every phrase with his fists and feet.

Bud quickly waded in and tried to pull Blip off the top of Mickey who was yelling loudly and battling to escape. Blip, however, had completely lost his temper after striving to keep his own fears and tension under control for so long. For a while things got quite nasty until Kall's wary comments and a change in the light made the boys freeze in mid tackle.

'Shh... boys... I think we have company again!'

Bud, Blip and Mickey untangled themselves and looked around in consternation. Blip and Mickey were looking very dishevelled and untidy, but in an instant the fight was over, the tension between them had all been released and the boys all surreptitiously moved closer together for support. Blip shook his ripped trouser leg to rid himself of a large amount of sand while he twisted his head around trying to see what held Kall's complete attention. The afternoon light had given way to cold, dark shadows and the breeze had dropped completely. The air was still, but menacing. Mickey shivered uncontrollably.

Kall was gazing at the forest edge while holding tightly onto the ponies' halters with one hand, making sure they did not escape. They started to whinny quietly in alarm and began fidgeting and scraping at the sand with their hooves. Kall had his crossbow loaded and had lined it up on Sage's back with his free hand. He was pointing it towards the nearby forest.

Bud was squinting in the enfolding darkness and staring with trepidation at the imposing, coniferous treeline.

Blip and Mickey slowly sank to the ground, so that they were almost hidden behind a sand dune topped with spiky marram grass. Bud joined them, but while the two boys hid completely from view, Bud peered carefully over the hillock and called quietly to Kall to check what was happening.

'Kall...?' Bud's stage whisper carried clearly in the empty atmosphere.

'I think it's the Nyxx – she's back again. I don't know how she got here so quickly – but she won't come out into the daylight.' Kall looked worriedly at the dark clouds slowly veiling the sky. 'She doesn't give up, does she? At least we won't see Merrick.'

'It isn't daylight any more Kall,' Bud observed tensely. 'What can she really do to us?' he enquired, not really wanting to hear the answer.

'She is all-powerful, a vagous wraith which cannot be destroyed. She carries the Subyx plague on her breath and she will seize your mind. She feeds on fear and other strong emotions.' Kall thought for a moment. 'Maybe Blip's recent anger directed her to us?'

'But you seem to suggest she is afraid of the light ... and cannot survive in the sun?' Bud queried hopefully, ignoring Blip's frightened moan.

'*She comes with the dark ... a black wisp of smoke – a hiss in the dark ...* whereas the *White Shadow* comes with the dawn *... and protects the very light of day.*' Kall seemed to be quoting again.

'Kall ...The White Shadow ... is that Uriel ... or maybe the horse - Aisling?' Blip called out quietly from his sandy hideout.

'I think both. They seem to be together – one doesn't exist without the other.'

'Two distinct parts of the same being?' suggested Bud.

'Yes I think so, but Uriel has protected you – or perhaps defended you – at least three times. I am thinking this problem is ours to overcome.' Kall suddenly tensed, 'Shh Quiet! Be still.'

'W-what is it?' Mickey tremulously chose this moment to speak up.

'I said quiet,' hissed Kall.

The inevitable, malevolent wisps of black smoke had started to swirl around a nearby tree. Loathsome tendrils stroked the spooked, quivering branches and twisted into tortuous shapes around the upright trunk which seemed to almost shudder in reaction. The sinister and diabolical female shape began to materialise and the hideous face and gaping mouth gradually came into focus. The black cavernous jaws started to speak incoherently. Disjointed and incomprehensible words reached the boys ears. The Nyxx started to hiss and spit venom as she drifted closer to the dunes where Blip and Mickey still lay shaking with fear.

Bud gulped, took a deep breath and went to stand beside Kall for support. His knees were shaking but he tried to pretend it was just the way he was walking through the thick sand. He stood with Kall behind Sage and helped to hold onto Scout's halter to try to stop him from rearing up and escaping along the now shadowy beach. Guru trembled but stayed close to Sage.

As the light became even more nebulous and almost disappeared completely, the Nyxx grew stronger and gradually materialised into the open – all the time wafting and gliding closer to the dunes. Her tainted, corrupted breath could be heard hissing in her throat like an angry snake. Kall slowly leaned over Sage's back and reached for his drum which was still slung carefully over the pony's withers. His hand stroked the skin gently and then beat out the soft rhythmic ostinato he had used earlier in the day. The steady rhythm representing hoof-beats could be heard throughout the cove. His other hand still remained holding his cross-bow steadily aimed at the approaching miasmic visitation of evil.

Bud started to mutter repeatedly under his breath, accompanying the steady tattoo on the drum which gradually became stronger and firmer as Kall discovered an unknown strength and obstinacy within him. The Nyxx wavered slightly. Her malevolent incantation had been interrupted by the rhythmic recital from the two boys. Her mouth gaped wider and the incoherent babble became strident and harsh – more threatening and aggressive than before. She punctuated each evil hex with a shriek of anger and the black eyes incessantly scoured and probed the beach, frantically seeking any glimpse of her stolen treasure. The smoke curled and writhed with poison as it snaked around the dunes and spewed over each hillock of coarse grass.

Blip and Mickey still lay shielded behind the dune, clasping their hands over their ears in the attempt to shut out the evil sounds getting closer and more strident with every passing second. Mickey was attempting to impersonate an ostrich – with his head almost concealed underneath a clump of grass and his face practically buried in the coarse sand. Blip however was starting to look around, wondering whether he could uncover the chest and ask for three wishes – or if they could all make their escape via the chest. Then he thought of Batty and Wayne and knew they had to defeat the wraith in some other way in order to give them time to arrive.

'Oh my God,' he muttered to himself. 'What if they appear now? They'll run straight into the Nyxx.' Blip poked his head over the top of the dune to find out what was going on ... and wished he hadn't. The smoky apparition was far closer than he expected. Kall was still drumming an anxious ostinato rhythm with his fingers and Bud was still muttering under his breath. Blip could just about hear 'Uriel' and 'wish' being repeated but the rest of it was indistinct. Blip looked on with horror as Kall stopped the drumming, placed both hands on the crossbow then aimed and fired straight at the heart of the Nyxx.

Bud and Blip cheered and applauded, and the gloom lifted for a second and then closed in with a deafening blast of thunder. The bolt shot straight through the wraith and disappeared into the inky blackness beyond. The Nyxx stood erect and powerful and sneered at the three boys, taunting and jeering at them with an incomprehensible screeching which they could only interpret as dire threats. She closed in on the boys and the first wisps of smoke started to twist around the ponies legs. The rancid foul smell set them all gagging and Kall and Bud had a hard time trying to control the panicked beasts.

Blip held his nose to ward of the foul smell while his eyes darted everywhere looking for the pebbles and stick that Mickey had so disdainfully kicked away. But he quickly realised they would have no effect if Kall's sharpened bolt couldn't inflict any damage. His eyes fell on Bud's rucksack with the long oilskin-wrapped item protruding from the top of the bag. What if they returned the item to the Nyxx – would it go away and leave them alone? Blip had no time to think, his free hand shot out and grasped the item – intending to pull it quickly from the rucksack and send it spinning towards the wraith hoping she would take it and back off, leaving them alone. Still holding his nose with his left hand, he grasped one end of the treasured item with his free right hand and a small part of the oilskin fell open.

The skies whirled – the heaven's roared and for a split second, Blip's heart and courage soared like a bird. He shouted out words and phrases incomprehensible even to his own inspired state of mind and he leapt to his feet, brandishing the long, yet supple item, high above his head.

He found himself grasping a white-hot metal handle, which scorched and scarred his hand and made him drop it quickly into the sand. A bolt of blinding white light shot straight up into the darkened sky and Bud and Kall whirled around in shock – not knowing what had caused the blazing light. Bud quickly took in the scene unfolding before his eyes. Blip was squirming around the sand dune holding his hand in agony. Mickey had appeared from his ostrich-like state and was staring with huge strained eyes at the long item now partly unsheathed and glowing with a bright incandescent beam of fire. A glowing, pulsating jewel-filled sword hilt was lying in the sand, with the rest of the sword still sheathed in the greasy oilskin.

The Nyxx shrieked again in sheer turmoil – and the outraged wraith, the overpowering rancid stench, and the portent of evil – all seemed to swoop over the sand dune at the same time. Mickey's eyes rolled in his head and he blacked out completely. Blip tried to run, the agony of his stricken hand completely forgotten by the overpowering sense of evil and disease. He tripped over the edge of the sand dune and rolled down the hillock where he lay still, trembling and shaking. He found himself close to the chest and quickly reached out and thrust his burnt hand through the sand until he could feel the comforting metal rim which bound the chest.

The ponies were plunging and rearing in horror and Kall had his hands full trying to keep them from escaping – but Scout and Guru fled from his outstretched hand before he could get a more secure hold on their halters. Sage circled round and round looking for safety and eventually followed the other ponies, forcefully dragging Kall with him as they all headed down the beach.

Bud was momentarily blinded by the glaring beam of light shining from the sword hilt but he could feel the sudden enraged approach of the Nyxx and he dived onto the blade while tugging at Blip's hanky where it still resided in his jeans pocket. He grasped the hilt while protecting his hand with the hanky and, trying to ignore the scorching heat; he drew the rest of the sword from the wrapping and then gazed in awe and wonder at the scintillating, golden flames shooting up and down the blade. He felt mesmerised by the beacon of power streaming from the glowing shaft and twisted around to see the effect it was having on the Nyxx. The demonic apparition was cowering low on the ground hiding those coal-black eyes from the blinding light.

Bud laughed out loud in relief, wielded the sword like a warrior of old and brandished it around his head before stabbing it straight through the heart of the smoky wraith. Lightning bolts burst from the blade and the sky shimmered with fire. The phantom folded in on itself and the Nyxx disappeared with a final scream of torment. A few smoky tendrils remained which dissipated as Bud cut and swiped with the sword until they too had disappeared. The clouds rolled back, the sun shone and he was left panting for breath while the other boys slowly returned to the dune and gazed in awe at the young warrior still holding aloft the most beautiful and powerful sword they had ever imagined.

CHAPTER NINETEEN

'Oh boy, oh boy – Wow!' Mickey's eyes glittered in sudden excitement.

'Oh bro that's wicked! Ow! Oh my God ...my hand hurts!'

'Shh – I can hear something.' Kall had his hand on his drum and could feel the vibrations through the skin. The boys all froze and Bud quickly hid the sword under the once discarded oilskin as the hilt could still be seen glowing red-hot. Sage, Guru and Scout all whinnied in welcome, as a pale horse trotted around the bend of the river and Aisling appeared carrying two very tired but relieved passengers (and a very disgruntled dog) on her back.

The majestic horse's sides were heaving with the effort of a fast gallop and she had foam on her flank. There was a struggle as the two children attempted to unwrap the struggling dog who had just realised her ordeal on horseback had come to an end. They eventually released her from the safety straps and then Bluebell leapt down and went berserk, running around the beach, barking excitedly and telling Aisling off. Batty released her own vice-like grasp of the beautiful white mane and scrambled down from her back, with Wayne not far behind. Bluebell suddenly caught sight of two familiar figures approaching, and went charging up to Bud and Blip, almost beating the high jump world record in her haste to lick their faces. Well – Bud's face anyway ... Blip's face was a lot nearer to the ground!

Aisling ignored all the excitement and bent her elegant head to drink from the clear waters of the river.

* * *

'Bud! Blip! Kall! Are you all ok?' Batty leapt at the boys in relief and Blip, for once, accepted her bear hug and returned it with interest. Mickey thumped Wayne on the back – the closest their family ever came to giving a bear hug!

'Ow! Watch out for my hand, Batty!' Blip quickly held his hand away from any contact with his exuberant sister.

'Sorry – what have you done to it?' Batty looked at Bud for an explanation as Blip had already turned and joined Aisling at the river to bathe his blistered hand in the cold, clear water. Batty froze into immobility. 'Bud ... Bud? W-what is that?'

Bud had returned to fetch the sword – enthralled by the burning tattoo in the palm of his hand. The others surrounded Bud as he held up the sword for them all to see. The once burning, flaming brand now had a normal, metallic sheen to it – but the bright jewels and quality of the engraving on the hilt still made them all gasp in awe. This wasn't a normal, everyday sword; this was one of a kind – unique and exclusive.

'Is this it? The treasure we were meant to find? The quest we were given?' Batty asked rather unnecessarily.

Mickey stretched out his hand in order to take it from Bud's grasp but Wayne stepped in and stopped him abruptly. 'No Bro – it is not ours. It's not our treasure Mick – look at it, it is not for the likes of us – it must belong to Uriel. He set the quest.'

'Oh give over Wayne, your brain is addled.' Mickey spat near Wayne's feet and stalked off towards the sand dune where the chest lay hidden.

Bud's eyes were still shining with the powerful effect of holding the sword but he regretfully placed it back in the oil-skin wrapping and stowed it back in the top of his rucksack. He then looked over at Blip still bathing his hand in the river. 'Blip – are you ok? We have to go now.'

Blip waded out of the river, patted Aisling and returned to the others still grimacing and holding his hand out as if he was carrying a priceless

Fabergé egg. Kall was still holding onto the ponies' halters but he indicated to Bud that he should follow Mickey to keep an eye on him. Bud nodded and picking up his rucksack he wandered over to the sand dunes.

Batty and Wayne went together to say goodbye to Aisling and the other ponies, both children finding it difficult to hold back the tears. Batty made sure she stroked and patted each of the ponies in turn and then tearfully went to hug Aisling standing patiently by the banks of the river. Wayne – not usually very demonstrative, touched Aisling lightly on the muzzle and then deliberately leant forward and stroked and kissed the glowing mane. As the two of them stepped back, the pale, almost shimmering horse reared up and set off back along the forest track with a faint whinny of farewell.

The boys and Batty said a regretful goodbye to Kall, hoping to meet again in the future –all except Mickey who was waiting sulkily near to the chest. Batty gave Kall a big tearful hug and gave him lots of messages to recite to Sula on his return. The boys shook hands more formally, clapped each other on the back and then eventually they couldn't help themselves, and copying Batty, they just hugged Kall in grateful thanks for all he had done for them while on Thelasay.

Kall collected the ponies together and then for safety, harnessed them to a nearby tree. He waited, while they uncovered the chest and wiped the lid clean of excess sand before opening it. Mickey and Wayne stood back, watching them nervously.

'Ok Batty, you and Wayne must go back first,' said Bud.

'I still can't believe we are out of danger,' Blip observed unexpectedly, still holding the palm of his hand while trying to hook his rucksack strap over his arm. He glanced around the bay – just in case.

Mickey suddenly stepped forward, his chin jutting out aggressively, 'I'm going first,' he said looking warily at the trees.

'Oh no you won't!' said Blip. 'Batty will go first with Bluebell ... and look ... Wayne is still really pale – he isn't fully recovered and he needs to get home. You can follow me.'

Batty stopped the impending argument by climbing quickly into the chest after unfolding the bracket to stop the lid from closing completely. 'It's ok Wayne – just follow me.' She tried to reassure the slightly harassed and white-faced boy and smiled kindly at him. Bud lifted Bluebell into Batty's waiting arms and she barked a couple of times as he lowered the lid. There was a bright flash which made them all blink and Batty and Bluebell were on their way. Bud reopened the chest and Wayne gasped when he realised he chest was completely empty.

'Wayne – you're next. Nothing to worry about – it's that simple.' Bud gave him a gentle push towards the chest. He then lined up Blip and Mickey and watched carefully while each boy climbed into the chest. He helped fold their arms and legs in and tucked their heads down as he closed the lid on each intrepid, but rather nervous, traveller. He had to give Mickey more than just a gentle push to get him in.

'We'll have to leave you here then Mickey,' Bud started to whistle impatiently as Mickey had started to back off but soon changed his mind at Bud's threat. He heard Kall laugh and practically leapt into the chest and pulled the lid down on himself before Bud could even check he was safely ensconced.

When it was his own turn, Bud called out to Kall, waved and looked regretfully at the beautiful beach and cove they were all leaving behind. Kall walked towards him and said with a slight break in his voice ... 'We must all go our separate ways, my brother – but with heart bound to heart. You will return – I am sure of it. Until then...!' Kall gripped Bud's forearm strongly and after blinking his eyes a few times, he let go.

'Heart bound to heart,' Bud repeated under his breath as he climbed into the chest, carefully tucking his rucksack, along with the wrapped sword, underneath his long legs. 'We *will* return Kall.' With one last fond look at Kall and an appreciative glance around the cove – he gently pulled the lid down over his head.

Kall spent a few minutes throwing sand over the lid of the chest and placed some Marram glass clods on the top to disguise it. Then he mounted his pony ... turned Sage in the direction of Mowl village and cantered off, with Guru and Scout following closely behind. He turned around three times to gaze at the deserted beach.

* * *

Batty surreptitiously lifted the lid – not sure what she would find at home. Bluebell immediately jumped out with her tail wagging furiously ... glad to be home. She almost squeaked in excitement and licked Batty's face before she could climb out of the chest. The lively dog then tried to climb back into the chest – ready for another adventure.

'Oh Bluebell, you have to hush! Shh!' Bluebell had started to bark but obediently went back to squeaking quietly while Batty struggled out of the chest. She quickly closed the lid again and went to open the playroom door but the house still seemed quiet and still. No-one was home. She checked the clock and it seemed only a few hours had passed – as Uriel had suggested.

'Wow,' she muttered to herself, but at that point she heard a faint sound from the chest and went to help Wayne who was looking very pale and clammy. He was obviously feeling dizzy and nauseous, but he climbed out with Batty's help. He still seemed to be very weak and he quickly sat down on a nearby comfy chair looking exhausted. Bluebell sniffed all around him and gave his dangling hand a quick lick, while Batty closed the chest lid once more.

Blip arrived with no problem except that Bluebell actually managed to get back in the chest with him, delaying his exit. Batty went to drag Bluebell away and prevented her from washing Blip's face with her long sloppy tongue.

'Aw Bluebell stop it. Leave me alone – I know I need a shower but...' At that point just as he was struggling to stand up Mickey arrived bang on top of him even though the lid had not been closed. Mayhem ensued. Bluebell really started to bark excitedly – even growling warningly at times. Batty tried to shut her up while Blip and Mickey tried to wrestle their way out of the chest.

'Ow … don't touch my hand! Get off me – you're hurting me you heavy lump! How did you get here so quickly? Let me get out of this chest – Bud will be here soon! Stop hugging me!'

Mickey wasn't too happy to find himself on top of Blip either … 'what the hell are you doing – stop hugging *me* you great ginger lump! Let me get out and stop your whingeing. Blip! I don't want to be so close to you … and get off my backside!' Mickey scrambled quickly out of the chest as if he was being chased by Merrick. Blip got out equally quickly in case Bud appeared before he could do so. Having Mickey suddenly appear on top of you in the chest, was like landing a smelly whale – but having Bud suddenly appear would be like grappling with a giant squid … all arms and legs!

Blip quickly shut the lid, while Mickey glared at him, shook himself off and stalked out of the side door in order to go home. Wayne got up out of his chair, holding his mouth as if he was about to be sick, and quickly followed his sulky brother out of the door. 'Thanks' … a low mutter could be heard followed by a lot of retching.

Batty looked concerned, but Blip chuckled. 'They'll be ok now. Let's hope the police aren't waiting for them.' Blip looked closely at Batty …'aren't you feeling sick?' he asked while moving his feet out of the target area.

'No, I'm ok this time. Perhaps I am used to it – or perhaps I had other things to think about this time and it took my mind off it. Oh here's Bud now.'

Bluebell started her usual greeting while Bud just sat there in the chest wondering where Mickey and Wayne were. 'Where are the Wilton's?' he asked worriedly looking all around the playroom.

'They are ok. They went off home without any thanks for fetching them back safely!'

'Blip, I think it was our – or rather *your* fault they ended up in Thelasay in the first place … and Wayne did say thanks anyway!' Batty defended her new friend.

Blip looked a little ashamed, 'but we got them back ok didn't we? And we solved Uriel's quest too. Oh Bud … the sword … where is it?' and Blip started to rub his blistered hand once again.

Bud unfolded himself with difficulty and clambered out of the chest then leant back inside to reach for his rucksack and the sword still safely strapped under the flap. He slowly and almost reverently pulled it out of the chest and undid the rucksack to free the *treasure*. He laid the sword (still in its oilskin sheath) on the top of the closed chest and looked all around to check with Batty.

'No-one home yet?' he asked referring to their parents.

'No. No-one around, they must still be out visiting. Look it's only been a few hours.'

Blip and Bud turned to look at the clock and both shook their heads in confusion and awe.

'Come on Bud ... undo the oilskin ... let's see it again.' Blip was still unconsciously, gently rubbing his hand.

Bud took a deep breath and carefully started to peel off the oilskin cloth that had been protecting the burnished, iridescent blade that lay beneath. The jewelled hilt appeared, punctuated by a gasp from Batty who, now she was up close, had never seen anything so beautiful and powerful before. Bud slowly removed the rest of the oilskin protecting the sword – his hands shaking with anticipation. Blip moved a little closer, holding his breath and still rubbing his hand in memory of the moment he had wielded such great power and fire.

The sword eventually appeared with a startling flash of golden fire and Bud quickly put it down and backed away from the flaming blade. Batty and Blip were both standing silent and in total awe.

CHAPTER TWENTY

'**M**y sword...' Uriel took the three of them totally by surprise as his lithe, youthful figure strode past them and immediately grasped the jewelled hilt which seemed to fit his hand like a glove – as if it had been made for him alone. He stood erect and held the sword up, the blade illuminating the golden streaks in his wavy blond hair. He smiled and turned towards his incredulous audience, his eyes flashing with fire and authority. He seemed to glow and radiate vitality.

'Is it really your sword?' Blip didn't mean to doubt Uriel's obvious proprietary actions – but he still felt bereft, as though something special had been removed from his own grasp.

'Blip...!' Bud interjected a warning, yet he too was remembering what it felt like to hold and possess the sword. That split second of ownership had left him with an eternity of memories.

Uriel smiled and leant the sword against the wall where it stood like a symbol of faith. Bud realised he was observing Uriel more closely as the significance of his actions re-triggered a few deeper thoughts and reflections.

'Blip … let me see your hand,' Uriel said quietly.

Blip found that he couldn't refuse and held out his injured hand for all to see. Batty started to murmur in concern at the scorched flesh. The blisters had burst and the red, angry skin was scarred and puckered. Blip couldn't stretch his hand out properly as it pulled too much on the tender flesh.

'Bud … let me see your hand too.'

Bud moved closer to Uriel and held his right hand out. He had used Blip's dirty hanky as protection, but the skin was still red and scorched – although it wasn't as bad as Blip's hand.

Uriel held both hands lightly then enclosed each fist within his own. After a second he released them and they opened their hands and gazed at them in stupefaction. Both injuries had almost disappeared. Almost – but not quite.

'Remember this, during those times when the world grows cold and dark
You have the sign of power and light – you are inscribed with the mark.'

'Ugh- poetry,' Blip tried to laugh it off as he was both embarrassed and confused, but Bud looked closely at his hand and then looked questioningly at Uriel.

'W-who – what are you?' he stammered.

'Now is not the time Bud … but you are starting to realise … yes?'

'But it's never the time Uriel,' observed Batty.

'Be patient – you *all* know and realise more than you think.' Uriel stretched his hands apart and said, 'A few days ago, I stood before you incomplete. You have helped me to become entire and whole again.'

'Can you tell us more Uriel? … Please?' Batty pleaded.

Uriel sat down near to the chest and invited the children to join him. Bluebell laid her heavy head on his knee and gazed adoringly at him … watching every move of his elegant hands as they reached to caress her ears. Then she sighed in blissful contentment, as he gently stroked the soft fur between her eyes … serenely blessing her forehead.

Uriel hesitated before he started his rather extravagant explanation. 'You have visited the Island of Thelasay … an island that lies between two worlds. It is a human world, but with a closer connection to the spirit world than is experienced here. In this world … I am Uriel and can only appear when requested or required. There … I exist as the white shadow – a spirit which protects and guards the villagers from the spirit of the night. Aisling is my companion and my escort through the wilderness and the dark forests.

My sword is my weapon *and* my shield. Without it – I can only defend my friends and startle my enemies. The sword makes me complete and with it – I can battle to preserve what is good and legitimate.'

'You say you can appear here when requested?' Bud looked at Uriel thoughtfully.

Uriel nodded. 'You knocked … whether it was your intention or not …

If you knock - I will answer, if you ask – I will bestow

I'll be there when you entreat me and all darkness overthrow.'

'Oh Uriel – please No!' Blip sighed heavily.

'Uriel … what is the Nyxx? And how did <u>She</u> manage to possess your sword?' Bud wanted to get everything straight in his mind.

'*She* is the dark shadow – I am the white shadow. Together we are opposites – the chiaroscuro spirits. We are a paradox in time.' Uriel stopped for a moment and took a deep breath.

'We knew she was searching for a fantastic and powerful treasure and aspired to own it. When we discovered that she yearned for the sword – it was kept hidden in the chest to keep it away from such a poisonous wraith … but in time, she discovered its hiding place. She dispatched her servant Merrick, under a cloak of darkness, and following her instructions he managed to trick me and steal both treasured items. The Nyxx appropriated the sword and Merrick was ordered to conceal the chest for many years – so that I was unable to use it. It was supposed to remain hidden in the dunes for so long that she would be able to claim ownership of the sword.'

'How could he see to hide it,' questioned Blip, thinking of the near sightless drudge.

'In those days, when he was younger – he could see fairly well. He was attacked by an eagle which clawed at him and damaged his right eye when he was attempting to hide the chest in the dunes. So he was stopped from burying it too deeply. When *She* realised that you three had discovered the chest – *She* punished him further by taking the sight of his left eye too.'

'Why would they want to hide the chest if they already had the sword, Uriel?' Batty stroked the lid of the chest and Bluebell gave a small reproachful woof.

'The chest is my portal from one world to another. I can still travel, but cannot do so easily, without a necessary and complex transfiguration, so she tried to stop me from using it.' Uriel looked at Bud who nodded his head slightly and surreptitiously rubbed his palm with his left thumb.

Uriel continued ... 'the chest was hidden in this world, so when it was found ... by you three ... I had to ask if you would attempt the recovery and so challenged you to fulfil an extra task during your visit to Thelasay. Remember I can only defend without the sword, so it had to be a quest undertaken by the physical and earthly world, rather than the spirit-led world. You had to solve the poem in order to take back the sword.' Uriel grinned suddenly at Blip. 'Luckily for me – you had already put yourself in the position of rescuers and I knew you wouldn't let a simple poem beat you!'

'So you sent *us* on the quest – to get *your* sword?' Blip was amazed and a little shocked.

'Only the best for the job,' grinned Uriel, 'but don't forget the little matter of two missing boys ... I seem to remember that being due to your misguided wish, Blip!'

Blip hung his head slightly.

Uriel then stated, 'You had to go anyway, in order to learn to take responsibility for your own actions – so I just requested that the extra task become part of the rescue. I made it clear to Batty that I wasn't insisting ... I requested.' He smiled again and said gently, 'your own free will made the decision.'

'But it was dangerous for us all Uriel ... and we nearly lost Bluebell too!' Batty held the dog close to her and Bluebell licked her nose in agreement.

'Try to trust me, all of you ... I was there to defend you and shield you from harm ... but I couldn't openly let you know that – it had to be down to your trust in me. I did hint at it ... remember – *I'll be there when you entreat me and all darkness overthrow.*'

'We kept hearing hoof beats and saw flashing lights, every time it grew a bit scary. Was that you and Aisling?' Bud asked.

Uriel nodded his head. 'Just two of the signs of the white shadow … something to look and listen for when you feel worried or stressed,' he advised, glancing at Batty.

'And … the brush of wings?' Bud didn't give up easily.

'Was that an owl? It was too big for an owl … you said Merrick was attacked by an eagle – was it an eagle?' Blip was eager and excited by the thought.

Uriel laughed. 'No …but …'

'… Now is not the time!' They all chorused in unison while Bluebell barked.

'Shush Bluebell!' again in unison.

Uriel picked up the old oilskin cloth and placed it in a nearby waste bin, then he carefully opened the lid of the chest and they all took a deep breath as they realised it wasn't empty. They all stepped forward to look. Lying in the base of the chest was a supple leather scabbard and belt, with the image of a rearing white horse embossed on the front. Uriel reached in and lovingly picked up the scabbard and belted it around him.

'Out with the old …' he indicated the oil cloth in the bin, '… and on with the new.' Then with one hand he held the opening of the scabbard and with the other he held the dazzling sword. He smiled at the flicker of flame running along the blade, and … slowly … slid it into the sheath and essentially – sent it home. '"Lift the supple, guarded sheath - And bring it to this timeless throne."' Uriel quoted his own verse without explanation. He looked around at the three children and Blip opened his mouth to ask a question but Uriel held up his hand to stop him.

'All questions will be answered in time. Be patient. Can I suggest that you might be more careful for what you wish for in the future?' They all vigorously nodded their heads.

'Uriel, you aren't leaving are you? Will we see you again?' Batty asked anxiously as her bottom lip began to quiver.

'And can we go to Thelasay again?' Blip requested.

'We are heart-bound to Kall and Sula,' commented Bud making up a new phrase as he did so. 'I hope we can see them and learn more about them?'

Uriel looked earnestly at the three hopeful faces. 'I can only say that you will need to keep watch. Keep a vigil and safeguard yourselves from the cold and dark.' He climbed carefully into the chest with one hand on the hilt of his sword and started to lower the lid. Bluebell immediately started whining and tried to climb into the chest to be with him. Bud hauled her back – but small whimpers kept emanating from deep within her throat. Batty took Bluebell from Bud and cuddled her as the tears rolled steadily down her own cheeks.

Uriel hesitated, smiled and pushed the lid back open again. He quickly slipped out of his fine white shirt revealing a muscular yet elegant upper body. 'Batty, take this. It may be comforting for Bluebell ... and all of you ... in all your darkest moments.' He handed his shirt to Batty who immediately held the soft material to her cheek while Bluebell sniffed at it with interest. Uriel glanced around at the three siblings. 'I am *proud* to be your companion and your ...' he stopped himself, hesitated and then smiled. 'Don't forget ... *The chest holds more than just one key.*' He grinned at them and bent forward, almost doubling over in order to make enough room ... and then gently shut the lid. *'Be vigilant for that scorching, spark of fire.'* There was a sudden flash and then silence. They all rushed over to the chest and opened the lid carefully. It was empty. He was gone.

They looked at each other over the top of the chest.

'What-what was that?' muttered Batty.

'His back ...what was on his back?' Blip gazed questioningly up at Bud, but his elder brother just looked intently at the chest and then at his siblings, nodding his head to himself as if realising he had been right. Blip tried again. 'Bud – what were those marks on his shoulders? It looked like something growing – it looked like – it looked ...' Blip faltered and stopped. He stayed silent for a while, just watching Batty holding on tightly to Uriel's shirt. 'And what did he mean ... "*The chest holds more than just one key?*"' Blip complained. 'He has said that to me before – what does he mean?'

'I think we will find out sometime Blip ... as long as we are "*vigilant for that scorching, spark of fire.*"' Bud mused thoughtfully. 'I think we already know about the marks on his shoulders. I just need to think it through methodically and work out the signs. We *do* know – I'm almost sure of it ... Let me think.'

'Oh I didn't say goodbye to Sula properly,' Batty suddenly cried out and Bluebell immediately tried to reassure her by licking her knees. 'Oh Bluebell thank you – but I'm all wet now,' she laughed.

* * *

'Hey! C'mon! ... Take-away! Take-away! Get it before it goes cold!' Antonio shouted through the door and made them all jump in surprise.

Blip decided he was suddenly very, very hungry and leapt for the door before Bud and Batty could move. He wasn't as quick as Bluebell though, and she nearly tripped him up in her haste to reach the hot food she could smell wafting from the kitchen. 'Argh ...Watch out dog! I need to get to the chop suey rolls before Bud can reach his tentacles across the table.'

'My what?' asked Bud suggestively!

'Don't be rude and uncouth you two!' Batty sighed, 'we're back to the suggestive comments again Bluebell!' She paused, 'But I bet you'd have loved playing with the stick and the two stones on that lovely beach.' Then she thought for a while ... 'We could name it Midway Cove ... midway between two worlds.' She nodded her head in acceptance of her own title, even though the others were already out of hearing range.

'Hands first, kids!' Antonia called out rather annoyingly, they thought.

'Kids! Mum I'm 14 – I've seen too much of life to be called a kid.' Bud objected while winking at the others.

Blip decided he wouldn't get his tea unless he washed his hands, so he made sure he was first. Bud quickly followed and Batty tried to squirm in between them to reach a small section of the sink. Blip turned his hand over while washing and froze. A red mark was still clearly noticeable and Bud watched him as he rubbed at it gently. He turned his own hand over to compare their marks and the boys both smiled at each other in companionable silence. Batty looked up at them, raising her eyebrows in mock disdain.

'The red hand gang rides again,' she said sarcastically.

'You're just jealous!' The boys chorused in unison.

'Jealous! I have no wish to pick up a red hot piece of metal and burn my hand so much that it blisters and leaves a mark!' Batty took the opportunity to slink away quickly while they compared their scars and she managed to get to the table and have first choice of chop-suey roll before they realised.

'Well you three ... how has your day been? Did the game go well? Have you had an exciting day?' asked their Dad, referring to the computer challenge they were supposed to have been running.

Husband and wife shook their heads sadly at each other, as the three of them laughed so much that Blip started choking on some rice. Bud smacked him on the back with one hand and waved his fork around uncontrollably with the other, so that a piece of chicken flew across the room. Bluebell hastily snapped this up and then looked very surprised as Batty joined her on the floor while laughing hysterically.

CHAPTER TWENTY-ONE

The three children were worn out and spent a calm and unexciting Sunday reading, playing computer games and occasionally standing totally still ... almost frozen in time, as they recalled various incidents which had occurred on Thelasay. They had grown to love the beautiful, rustic island and felt a pang of sadness as they remembered their new-found friends in the village. The feelings of deprivation were even more enhanced when they considered the absence of security and the sense of refuge they had experienced with Uriel. This was very disheartening and Batty could often be heard muttering ... *This – the shield-arm of Thelasay ...* whenever Bud and Blip saw her wandering aimlessly around the house.

Bluebell was exhausted, but managed to catch up on some sleep, happily snuggled up in her basket which now contained Uriel's shirt. Her nose was tucked right inside the shirt, but the children noticed she still growled occasionally and twitched uneasily in her sleep.

* * *

Monday dawned all too soon for the *Santorini Swashbucklers* – a name chosen by Blip after a couple of night's rest in a soft bed. He had already forgotten the branches, the twigs and the mud huts and had spent Sunday trying to forget the dark, evil apparitions that still haunted his waking moments. He came up with the name as a reaction to all the black memories and wanted something light-hearted to forge new experiences and memories. It didn't help when Bud and Batty tried to make other suggestions.

'*The "B" Brigade,*' suggested Bud, but Blip thought this was a bit boring!

'How about the V*agabond Voyagers?*' said Batty? 'It's about time we used another letter of the alphabet!'

The banter continued over breakfast until "O" and "A" ... not understanding everything that was going on; decided it was time for them to catch the school bus. 'Come on you lot, out you go ... time to cheer up Mr. Gamble. Don't forget to go to your piano lesson on the way home Batty, and Blip don't forget to take your trumpet, you have a lesson today.'

'Aw Dad – can't I give it a miss today. I'll have to go and fetch it from upstairs.'

'No Blip ... It is orchestra tonight after school so you will need it anyway. I will come and pick you up at 5.'

'Yes Dad.' Blip dragged himself back up the stairs.

'Da-ad?' asked Batty in a pretend whiny voice.

'No you can't!' said "O" even before Batty had even stated what she wanted.

'Dad, that's not fair ... Dad ... we started African Drum lessons at school last week and it's really cool.' She continued ... 'Can I have an African drum and then attend some lessons after school?' She hurriedly added, 'It's not on a Monday so it won't affect my piano lessons. It's really good – you can use them to send messages.'

Blip and Bud glanced knowingly at each other. They both thought this was a good idea – but didn't think Batty was going to get anywhere with her request.

'We could all learn,' she indicated the boys as well.

'So – you would be practising out loud, in all the corners of the house?' Antonia asked with some trepidation.

'No Mum – we could keep them in the playroom and shut the door.'

'Them?'

'Well we will fight over it if we only have one,' Batty said reasonably.

'Come on – off to school,' the long-suffering parents had heard enough. 'We will think about it and discuss it at teatime.'

'OK thanks Dad!' And with that, the Santorini Swashbucklers scrambled out of the house.

They were early enough to grab the bench before Mickey and Wayne had appeared, so they all settled down comfortably to await the bus and the arrival of the *Wandering Wilton's* ... as Blip had entitled their errant neighbours. Wayne and Mickey arrived panting as the bus chugged its way up the slight incline. Mickey was looking sulky and sullen, hardly even acknowledging their presence – but Wayne smiled fondly at Batty and went to sit beside her to talk about their return home and how their parents had reacted.

The bus arrived and interrupted their conversation, just as it was getting to the interesting part about what the local community police officer had said. Batty leapt excitedly onto the bus with the others, as she was looking forward to talking with her new friend, Lenka, but the seat was empty – there was no Lenka looking shyly at her new friend, instead there was only Francine and Raine smirking nastily. Batty went to sit down as far away as she could manage, but could still hear their loud whispers. Bud and Blip leapt on board to meet up with their respective friends and didn't notice Batty's heartache and loneliness.

'Can I sit with you Batty?' Wayne's quiet voice could still be heard over the clamour of the rest of the children.

'Y-yes – are you sure Wayne? You go to the big school, it will look funny.'

'But you are my friend. You looked after me ... now it is my turn.' Wayne sat down and gave her arm a little friendly nudge. After talking closely to Batty on the island, he had begun to realise that although she seemed strong and obstinate, she was sometimes lonely and vulnerable. Batty smiled tremulously at him and brushed away a small tear which ran down one smooth cheek. Wayne spent the entire journey making her laugh at the tales he was telling of their return home; how Mickey had made up a few melodramatic stories to explain to their parents just why their uniform was in such a state; why they were so tired; where they had been, etc. etc. They laughed so loudly that Francine and Raine became aware of their enjoyment and closeness and they looked on with astonishment and distaste.

When they all started to disembark from the bus Frankie and Raine tried to push into Batty – but Wayne was standing in the way pretending to wait for Mickey. They took one quick glance at Wayne and decided to leave it and wait for another chance later in the day. They got off the bus and ran quickly into the school looking back over their shoulders at Batty, who was linking arms with her brothers and smiling affectionately at Wayne. Mickey however, was still scowling and sulking at his own brother's betrayal which didn't go unnoticed by the two girls who were already plotting their next spiteful campaign.

Blip and Bud traipsed into the senior section of the school with their usual pals and were met at the entrance by a smiling Mrs. Cresslyn.

'Mrs. Cresslyn … er hello,' Blip hesitated.

'Ricki … er Blip hello. I hope you have completed your homework this time?'

'Er yes Miss … Er what homework – oh … that homework …y-yes Miss – of course I have done it!' Blip looked questioningly at Sandy and Stu, but they just held their hands out and shrugged. The friends passed into the school arguing about what the homework should have been, but if they had looked back they would have seen the unusual sight of Mrs. Cresslyn licking her finger and swiping the air in triumph.

'One up to me I think,' she turned quickly and grinned at Mr. Gamble who was already looking harassed and careworn … and it was only Monday.

Bud ambled into the school with his own pals, all smiling widely. They were pleased to see Mrs. Cresslyn smiling and laughing and hoped her husband, Prof. Cresslyn was in a similar good mood.

The day went well for Bud and Blip. Everything had reverted to normal. Mrs. Cresslyn was ready for Blip, Dr. Cresslyn was as strict and suspicious as usual and Mr. Gamble strode around the school with the weight of the world on his shoulders. If he had known that one of the *Santorini Swashbucklers* was watching him with concern and was considering making a wish for him to 'cheer up and have a good laugh' he would have resigned on the spot and referred himself to the hospital with a nervous breakdown.

Wayne, usually sullen and sulky like his older brother, was showing signs of smiling and laughing and was feeling more confident within his own circle of friends. He even went so far as to try to coax a smile out of his bad tempered brother when he met him in the corridor at break time. Mickey however was feeling embarrassed and angry about what had happened over the weekend. He had been tempted to explain to his parents and the police officer, just what had occurred – but for once, had allowed himself to be persuaded by his younger brother who had realised that it would actually be more sensible if he kept quiet. Mickey had done as his brother had suggested, but on reflection, he wasn't feeling happy about it.

Batty wasn't faring so well. She had spent the morning on her own, trying to avoid Frankie and Raine but they had managed to catch up with her at lunchtime and were now making up for it with their comments. It didn't help that a new girl had started that day and had immediately made friends with the two girls. Karli Nixon had already joined the other two girls in making her life hell. Batty found herself wishing that Lenka was there to talk to and that she had some support. A couple of the other girls had tried to be nice, but had backed off when the three spitfires (Batty's terminology) had threatened to make their lives a misery too.

She wished she was near the chest so that she could make a wish three times. Batty knew she shouldn't, but thought that surely, this might be one of the times when it could be considered to be appropriate. She hoped that Lenka hadn't left the school ... she had only been there for one day, but already they had become firm friends. Batty shivered and pulled her coat on as the day grew suddenly cold and the sky darkened.

'Scatty Batty – Scatty Batty!' the repeated harsh whispers got louder and closer. Batty turned slowly to find the three of them lined up in front of her.

'On your own again, Batty?' asked Francine pointedly.

'No-one wants to be with you, do they?' Raine added cattily. 'The sky's getting darker – going to rain soon; must be because you are so depressed and so lonely ... ha!' Raine opened her mouth to attempt a few more comments.

'Well at least it's not going to *Raine* on my parade!' countered Batty quickly.

'Huh?' Neither Raine nor Frankie understood so they just pretended to laugh.

'No-one's going to want to be with you when I have finished with you!' Karli stated threateningly. There was a sudden silence and even Frankie and Raine looked uncomfortably at Karli. Batty held her ground as the girl stepped forward into her personal space and sneered at close range. She tried to meet Karli's aggressive stare – but found she had to look away from the dark, almost blank stare she encountered. There seemed to be no emotion behind the eyes and Batty found herself glancing around for some support. Frankie and Raine had also started to back off, not wanting to get involved with the newbie who was already challenging the pecking order and intending to make a grand impression on her first day.

Bud was watching Batty from the other side of the campus. He could see that she was clearly upset and that three other girls were approaching her and making her even more uncomfortable. The day had grown cold and dark and Bud watched while Batty shivered and pulled her coat on over her shoulders. One of the girls went right up to her and rudely stared at her.

'What's the matter Bro – what are you looking at?' Blip appeared at his elbow and looked in the same direction as Bud's finger. 'Oh ...not again ... Oh Bud! I wish we could do something to help.'

'I wish we could too, Blip ... I wish she had a good friend to rely on.'

A brilliant spark of light momentarily lit the area and was reflected off every window and glass door. Crystal flashes dazzled all the children who had gone outside after their lunch and Bud, blinking rapidly, saw Batty leap to her feet in amazement and rush to hug a petite, fair-haired girl who also looked really happy to see Batty.

'Hi Batty ... sorry I wasn't on the bus this morning, I had a dental appointment.' Lenka smiled widely at Batty and ran to meet her friend. She sensed Batty was upset and looked around at Francine and Raine who were backing off around a corner ... and then at the new girl Karli, who was standing her ground and laughing nastily as she witnessed the friendly greeting between the two girls.

'And you are?' asked Lenka in a friendly manner.

'Karli ... Nixon ... who are you?' Karli almost spat the words out.

'My name is Lenka – it means light,' Lenka smiled at the scowling girl 'I am Batty's friend.

'Oh she's got one then?' Karli sniggered and walked off in disdain.

Bud and Blip were watching carefully from the other side of the campus and started to relax and smile.

'She is ok now; she has her new friend with her.' Bud sounded relieved.

'Who's the other girl – the aggressive one? I've not seen her before,' asked Blip.

'Not sure ... Batty will need to watch that one,' Bud sounded disconcerted and a little puzzled.

'Bud ... did we just make three wishes?' Blip questioned. 'What caused that flash ... and how did Batty's friend arrive in such a timely fashion?'

Bud realised he had been rubbing the palm of his hand and looked at Blip. 'Maybe we did. Blip have you still got your dirty hanky with you?'

'Ooh ... yes ... sorry.' Blip slowly pulled the feculent piece of cloth out of his pocket.

'Well I can't answer your questions about the wishes; we are just going to have to go with the flow. *"Now is not the time"* ... as we have often been told.' Bud grimaced and added, 'But I really think you should get that monstrosity washed!'

'Well it seems we are still being looked after ... protected ... or safeguarded anyway?' Blip smiled and started rubbing unknowingly at his own hand.

'Guarded may be more appropriate.' Bud walked off slowly heading back towards his friends and left Blip pondering his words.

The day passed fairly quickly and Blip soon headed off to his orchestra practice with Sandy who played trombone. A large section of students aimed for the pavement outside school to wait for the school buses to take them home. Mr. Gamble was on duty and eyed the approaching hordes with a sigh. He lined them up, almost in single file and waited impatiently for the bus to arrive.

Bud and his friends Michaela and Pete were at the front of the queue, standing close to the sighing and despondent head teacher. Levi played the violin in the orchestra and was missing from the line-up. Batty and Lenka were almost at the back of the queue as the youngsters often got pushed around at home-time and Wayne was standing nearby with Mickey who was still scowling. Batty thought his face was more lined than usual and that so many frowns and sulks had seemed to have a negative effect on his usually full shiny face. She realised that Mickey looked pale and drawn.

Frankie and Raine queued up behind them, but for once they were also a little subdued as Karli had followed them into the queue even though she didn't even catch the school bus.

Karli smiled brightly at Mickey and started to engross him in conversation. Mickey cheered up a little with the attention, but Wayne moved away and went to join Batty and Lenka.

'Who is she?' asked Wayne.

'Her name is Karli Nixon ... she may be trouble, Wayne.' Batty warned him.

'I can tell,' Wayne shuddered. 'I don't like her eyes ... they are so dark.'

Their bus appeared, moving quite quickly around the bend as it was late again. Then as it started to move nearer the pavement outside the school gates ... Karli suddenly approached Batty without any warning and pretending to trip, she started to push Batty quite aggressively into the road. Lenka quickly leapt forward – her eyes flashing with a steely fire.

'Oh! No you don't ... not on my patch!' and she blocked Karli's advance with her small but wiry body and issued a direct challenge with her scorching eyes.

'Watch out!' warned Wayne as he realised the bus was still moving quickly and had only just started to brake. A disaster was averted; Mr. Gamble grabbed Karli Nixon by the arm, and pulled her away from the other children to impart some very strong words.

The kids all piled on the bus as soon as the doors opened. Bud raced to his seat and then watched carefully to check that Batty was safe and secure with her new found friends. He sat staring perplexedly at his young sister who was still standing alone on the pavement. Mickey, Frankie and Raine had all gone up to the top deck, but Wayne and Lenka had just climbed aboard and were sitting near the front of the bus waiting for her.

Bud hesitated and almost disembarked to find out what was wrong. Batty was staring in puzzlement at Karli's retreating back. Bud watched her carefully as she shook herself and followed Wayne and Lenka onto the bus, sitting quietly beside her friends and listening distractedly while they exchanged comments about their school day. They both kept glancing at the silent Batty, hoping she hadn't been too badly affected by the show of violence aimed towards her at the school gate.

'Hey sis ... everything ok? Bud called down the bus.

Batty turned and waved reassuringly at Bud. She mouthed the words, 'talk to you later,' and sat staring out of the window, contemplating what had just happened. She recalled dark, black eyes ... a faint, almost imperceptible aroma ... and implicit threats. She felt uncomfortable and ill at ease, but she wasn't sure why.

Batty heard Wayne and Lenka laugh together. They were trying to include her in their conversation and then Lenka shook her head in disbelief at one of Wayne's far-fetched stories. Batty became immobile and stared fixedly at her friend. Her fair, almost blond hair had isolated shiny golden threads of fire running through it – waving and swirling with each flourish of her head.

A bell clanged in Batty's mind. She had witnessed that before? Where? Words came unprompted into her memories ... *Be vigilant for that scorching, spark of fire ...* and ... *This – the shield-arm of Thelasay*

Had she missed the signs?

ABOUT THE AUTHOR

Gilly Goodwin is an author, music teacher and composer ... (using the name Gilly Goldsmith). She composes choral works/ original carols/ some sacred works/ songs and TV themes. She lives with her husband in Southport (UK) and has two grown-up children. She loves all animals – particularly dogs and has recently owned two springer spaniels – Holly and Jazzy.

URIEL ... A Whisper of Wings was influenced by a fascination with the conversations between C.S. Lewis and J.R.R. Tolkien where they discuss the hidden messages in their novels and argue whether they should be deeply hidden in the text or made more obvious to the reader.

Gilly has been writing and composing for a number of years, but this is her first (middle grade) novel and is intended to be part of a trilogy.

Coming soon .... Look out for the second and third novels in the trilogy.

URIEL ... A Flash of Fire
The second novel in the trilogy – continues the story of the sword.

URIEL ... A Prophecy of Angels
The third novel in the trilogy – focuses on the *Shield-arm of Thelasay.*

A more detailed website focusing on Gilly's writing and composing is under construction.

I hope you enjoyed 'A Whisper of Wings' and that you are intrigued by the presence of Uriel.

Please leave me a review.

Thank you
Gilly Goodwin

28214764R00111

Printed in Great Britain
by Amazon